THREE GLASSES OF WINE

HAVE BEEN REMOVED FROM THIS STORY

A

NOVEL

MARIAN MICHENER

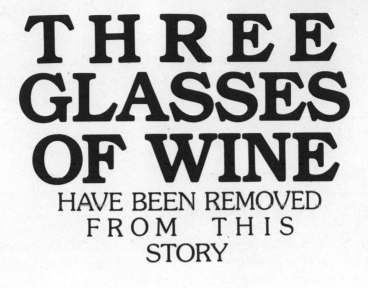

Silverleaf Press
Seattle, Washington

Printed in the United States of America.

Published by Silverleaf Press, Inc.
        P.O. Box 70189
        Seattle, WA 98107

We gratefully acknowledge Jean Swallow and Spinsters/Aunt
Lute for permission to reprint excerpts of an earlier version of
this novel which appeared in *Out From Under: Sober Dykes
and Our Friends*, ed. by Jean Swallow (Spinsters/Aunt Lute,
1983; $8.95; P.O. Box 410687, San Francisco, CA 94141)

Library of Congress Catalog Card Number: 88-061334

ISBN: 0-941121-00-3

First edition, September 1988

ACKNOWLEDGEMENTS

Heartfelt thanks and appreciation to these people who inspired this novel, read it in various stages, responded to it, believed in it and made it better:

Jean Swallow, Michael Rubin, Leo Litwak, Jean Miller, Kit Sturtevant, Chris Farrington, Diane Navicky, Danae Steele, Pam Cooper, Kit Junge, Carol Sterling, Roseanne Clark, Joyce LaGow, Lisa Maynard, Caitlin Sullivan, Brenda Weathers, Kate Miller, Nancy Emery, Marcella Benson-Quaziena, Rose Woodward, Sarah Gage, Karen Sterling, The Sister Gin Bridge Club, Cheryl, Mary Whisner, Jim Woods, Ann Larson...

And the countless invaluable friends, coworkers and family members who cut me a great deal of slack so I could do this.

*To Jean,
who fights
with me*

THREE GLASSES OF WINE
HAVE BEEN REMOVED
FROM THIS STORY

CHAPTER ONE

The fedora Brooke had given me, still crusted with volcanic dust, hung on the mirror. Neither of us would touch it after the summer night we'd come home laughing through the blizzard of ash, bandanas over our noses like outlaws. If something had melted and moved through us that night, it had hardened to moonscape by morning. She was sulking by then and said I hadn't cared for her gift. I asked wasn't my head more important than a thirty-dollar hat, and she said I'd missed the point. I guess she was right about that. I still don't get it. But the fate of the slouch hat reminds me that we were between disasters in Portland that October of 1980. The mountain was quiet, the plague undreamed of. Reagan was gaining in the polls; and we exchanged understanding looks with faggots, witches and Jews on the street about how bad things could get. It was an uneasy time.

And something different was happening inside my life, the kind of change that has so much to get around, it has to start quietly, like the end of a romance, or the beginning. It's hard to say where the first shift of feeling comes, but one thing leads to another and by the time you're ready to make your declaration, you're just catching up with what's already been settled. And you're standing there like a fool thinking you get to decide whether to stay or go, when in fact your baggage is already checked.

At the time, I didn't see how things would ever be different. On the contrary I felt set back every morning. That particular Sunday, for example, I'd been dreaming under a ton of lizards. And when I popped up in the thin air of white sheets, it looked like I was going to have to evolve all over again. My feet were primordial ooze. If I could blaze a path from there to my faithful head, I could invent civilization and get a cup of coffee. But I was stuck in the jurassic swamp somewhere around my knees and I didn't think I was ever going to make it home.

I took heart when I recognized the painting on the wall, a woman with a piece of fruit in her hand. It suggested that we were up past Genesis, a couple of millenia further along than I had thought at first.

Still, I told myself, this really wasn't going to do. I couldn't keep taking myself apart and putting myself back together again. One of these days all the king's horses and all the king's men were going to meet their match.

I swore off drinking. As always. Not in search of luxuries like clarity or self-knowledge, but from the cold certainty I'd be brain dead in another year if I didn't. In fact the mausoleum ceiling trim of the white victorian bedroom made me wonder briefly whether I might be dead already. My hair smelled ashy and everything tasted of ripe formaldehyde. But with a headache like I had, you know you're not dead. You just wish you were.

It was going to take me some time to reconstruct where I was and who I was with. But even then I knew she was mad.

Our bodies were back to back like a pair of plucked swans, her worn rayon nightgown clammy against my skin in a familiar way. Her spine had turned to concrete in the night. My eyes hurt. But the thin light reassured me that I was still in Portland with the Willamette throwing gray sun into the gray sky outside Brooke's polished windows.

Which brought me to the provocative question of how I came to be there. Hadn't I been about to die on the Hawthorne bridge in the middle of the night? Alone because we fought and I left her downtown. Walking across the bridge where anything could happen, so high above so much nothing, it was enough work just keeping the dark water in its place. Red lights, bells and barriers fell in front of me and it seemed I'd wandered hapless and drunk into the teeth of the drawbridge. It had taken all I could muster to run under the flimsy wooden arm. I walked on as relieved as a smuggler safe across the border, only to be surrounded again by lights and bells and the cranking mechanism. What I had passed was just the first barrier. I was on the tilting center. Well, I couldn't really tell if it was tilting yet or not, but I was too messed up to turn around, so I had to run on yelling, "stop," like a flea on a camel's back. The night and the city pounded even after I made it across the moving plates and under the gate to the solid side. I touched my chest then and blinked at the tear smeared sidewalk. But my grateful manner faded to casual in the few blocks between there and the tavern, The Other Side of Midnight.

The Other Side, that's where Brooke had come back in. She said she'd come to drown her own sorrows and she looked at everything except me at first. But after ruffling and pouting a bit, we wound up dancing and melting back together again. She danced with a hot formality that always made me laugh and want to take her home. She could be so tender when the music was slow and my aching ribs were the only ones close enough to hear. And she still had the longest shoulder blades I had ever run my hands down. I felt her heart beating under my face. Or

13

was it my heart? She didn't want to let me go. I hadn't wanted to resist in the first place. We must have called a cab.

So what was I doing Sunday morning still lying there wondering what to apologize for? I looked through the tendrils of the asparagus fern. The green eye of the elephant plant stand stared back. I liked Brooke's quirky furniture, though for myself I preferred mobility, which she would call downward mobility and claim she was not impressed. Still, I figured she must have liked my style; she'd stayed, hadn't she? But what good was staying if she was only going to hold herself away from me?

I reached back for her hip. It froze like a hunted rabbit. I let my fingers fall along the smooth top of her leg. At this point, I would always wish we could skip the argument and let the storm break into sex instead. But she contracted a breath further. And all I could think of to do was to lie there and count how many Sunday mornings I had spent trying to remember what I'd done Saturday night.

My first lover, Alison, used to wake up angry because I'd thrown up when things got twirly. Or I'd fallen asleep in the middle of things. I'd say I'd fallen asleep. She'd say I passed out. Alison had not been a drinker, bless her. Brooke was as likely to wind up under the table as I was. My hand spanned Brooke's muscled thigh, half the size of Alison's. I took into account the PreRaphaelites hanging on the wall, tasted my teeth and reminded myself that this was a different time.

With Brooke I was usually in trouble for flirting. Things offended her that used to just make Alison laugh. But this particular morning I was sure I hadn't touched or even looked at anyone else. It was the one thing I'd kept track of. Because we'd argued that afternoon in the light that swayed over the pool table, her saying I couldn't help myself and me saying I could. Though I had to admit that I sometimes found myself in the middle of a longing look not knowing how I got there. I assured her I could take care of myself.

She rested her chin on her cue and said she hoped so because she was running out of faith. That made me stand up and look at her. Those were not words Brooke used lightly. She was an ex-nun, with traces of neat creases even in her jeans. I'd never had much faith to lose. But I knew it was a pretty big deal with her. I mean, if she would leave God over this thing, she could damn well leave me.

The soft grin she gave me when she saw I understood threw the rest of my game off. But she got my attention. And she turned out to be the most interesting woman wherever it was that we went that night. I pretended I'd never heard her stories before and found her really quite charming.

If I hadn't had a point to prove, I might have flirted anyway. Because it turned us both on. Flirting and brandy were my favorite things because of the way they clear your head and veins and soul of anything else in no time.

Of course, Brooke was supposed to be the most important thing. And she hated it when I'd lean back in my chair and say it was cold ale and a card game that made life worthwhile. It reminded her of her Polish uncles whom we were supposed to be better than. I had always hoped not to have to be as good as my Quaker aunts. Brooke and I were different that way, among others.

What really troubled her about my libations to good friends and good times was that I lacked the proper sense of urgency about us shackling ourselves to our desks and earning our immortality.

Still, I didn't think that was what had pissed her off somewhere between Saturday night and Sunday morning. I pressed on in my investigation. I sat myself down in the bentwood rocker and cross examined myself:

"Can you account for your movements last night?"

"No."

"Did you discuss anything sensitive with the plaintiff?"

"I don't know. It seems like everything is sensitive these days."

15

I didn't have a clue what it was this time. So I gave up and got up even though my bones ached and I felt like I was bumping my head on something that wasn't even there. In the kitchen, I found to my relief that the marigold wallpaper had calmed down the crazy flickering dance it had been doing the night before. My eyes still crinkled. I scraped the pot across the burner loudly enough to let her know I was there. I warmed up some coffee to pour brandy in. I wanted to steel my nerves in case I was forced to leave her in self-defense.

Brooke had a skinny body, thick wire rimmed glasses and the face of a Raggedy Ann doll. But sometimes she moved like a dove taking flight. Church, school and the convent combined had failed to teach her humility, thank god. When she entered the kitchen, hipbones first, in her red satin dressing gown, she was all tall grace and obstinance, and I fell for her all over again.

But she startled a roach and her first words were, "Kill it."

That imperious tone of hers always made me go slack. The roach ran between my rooted feet. And my first words were, "It won't make any difference."

I hadn't wanted to start out this way.

She said, "You're on their side," with a petulant face that made me want to shake her. But it was safer to take it as a joke, pour brandy into her cup to sweeten her up, and wave my fingers as antennae in agreement with her.

She said, "Don't you care about anything?"

I stopped myself from saying, "What does that mean?" Because I knew she'd only say, "What do you think it means?" And I'd be back where I'd started, which come to think of it I was anyway, trying to figure out what was really bothering her. I was afraid I'd compound the offense if I admitted I didn't even know what it was.

I gave up looking for a response because she'd gone back to the bedroom where she was putting on her good blue jeans and a gray cashmere sweater so soft it could evaporate. Or maybe I got the feeling something was about to evaporate from my own inability to grasp the situation. Apparently, even though we were barely speaking, we were on good enough terms to go to breakfast. Which drove me crazy, her being willing to go out in public when things were so unresolved. But it usually helped if I went along. Some people, if you just leave them alone, can't stand to stay unreasonable. And Brooke was a very disciple of the goddess of reason.

She threw me a white silk blouse and a brown velvet vest of hers I liked to wear. I've always worn my lovers' clothes. For all I knew, I'd have gone naked if I hadn't had someone. Brooke did magic with thrift stores and found more pleasure in clothes than anyone I knew. Sometimes I thought I was one of her bargains, quality material but not very well taken care of, good stuff cheap.

Walking into the dining room at the Benson confirmed my feeling that nothing ever changes. I'd swear the same piano player had been playing "As Time Goes By" there for thirty years. Linen tablecloths, crystal chandeliers,it was not the kind of meal I would expect to alter the course of my life. I still couldn't recall the detail from the night before that had started this fight. With Brooke it was usually details. She said that was where the truth was told.

The food was piled on our plates like evidence. Brooke's blue eyes were cold as the champagne. When I caught my headache worried baby face in the silver spoon, I thought I looked more like the corpse than the murderer in this mystery. And the way my hair had grown out in rowdy black waves almost as long as Brooke's pretty curls spoke to me of how our bodies ran together sometimes. Which left me feeling put out of my own when she closed her wounded mouth against me.

Sometimes on mornings like this I would get the spooky feeling I'd married the wrong woman. That there was another one destined to make me happy. And she was waiting even now on a deserted streetcorner downtown looking at her watch and despairing of me. I thought I should excuse myself, stand up, fold my napkin on the table, walk out and go find her. And take her arm and go home with her and sleep off this bad dream of a life. But instead I looked at the incremental waltz of the sweep hand on my own watch and made a game of counting how many times in an hour I could charm the hostess into filling my glass. Which left me there with the same old long-limbed woman and her riddle. And I could see the claws I was going to have to get past before I could rest my head on her feathers.

When the first sip of champagne hit, so did the memory of my fist coming down on the blue hood of the Porsche that had cut in front of my pub crawl the night before. I called the guy a bastard and he called me a bulldyke, thank you very much. When he opened his door, we had to run up the alley with several Irish coffees sloshing in our brains. Brooke tottered on those rattan shoes I had told her not to wear in the first place. But it had been an adventure. Or so I thought. I laughed. Brooke closed her face like a bank vault. She looked as if she'd never seen me before. You'd have thought I had hit her instead of the car.

Then she kissed me against the brick wall, so I assumed we were reconciled. But maybe this all happened earlier. I couldn't remember whether we had made love in the end, which was odd considering we had been stroking each other's thighs all night. From how bloodless her mouth was across the breakfast table, I decided we hadn't. Maybe that was the tiff. All I could definitely remember was the key in the lock, the door opening, the marigold wallpaper wavering in the light.

I floated a strawberry across the top of Brooke's champagne. She looked pleased as she put it in her mouth so I thought I had a chance. I said, "I give up."

She gave me a deliberate blank look.

I said, "What did I do?"

Had I patted a friend on the ass? Invited someone over for an indecent cup of tea? Whatever it was, I was sorry. I felt like I was conceding the fight. But I wasn't surprised that she took in a breath and set her thin shoulders like she was just getting started. "You didn't do anything."

"What did I say then?" Now I was getting somewhere.

She took off her glasses. Her pale blue eyes diffused before they could reach me. She quoted me to myself like my own deadly gospel. "You said, 'Monogamy is always the same.' "

I wanted to laugh, but I clutched my wrist and lowered my face remembering my head was on the block. Surely, even dead drunk I had more sense than to say such a thing. I said, "Nonsense. When?"

She said, "Last night. Just before you fell asleep on me."

Arguing I'd been dreaming or talking in my sleep would have only made it worse. Not remembering didn't help; and denial was useless because she always knew what she knew. But just as I was running out of indefensible positions, something different happened. She put her glasses back on. Her eyes met mine again. She sighed and said, "It doesn't matter."

I was stunned. It wasn't like Brooke to let a point pass. I took note that her surgical edges hadn't had their usual sparkle all day. A warning prickled in the fog at the back of my head. It was this weariness of hers that was really dangerous. When she let up, I saw that it never was what I did or didn't do that mattered. It was that she thought I didn't love her.

For my part, I'd always said I always would. I believed that. Except I couldn't get my heart to move the way you'd think it would.

I used the image of our first night together to bring the feeling back. Not even so much finally kissing on the rain splashed porch, her saying she'd had too much to drink and me claiming I didn't know what she meant. And I never could believe it had been just one silken kiss, it had felt so kaleidoscopically packed with kisses to come. But earlier, she had filled my glass, and I had felt my skin sparkling where her eyes touched me. And I had seen how I was as thirsty for her as for the first taste of champagne.

I sipped and reminded her. She smiled. But from a distance.

"I really love you," I said, borrowing against my intention to make it true. "There's nothing more important to me."

I could see it was fifty-fifty with her whether to believe me. And I felt just as mixed to tell you the truth. I kept my eyes on her while she wavered, because that's what we always did. But, while I waited for her to decide, I counted on the hand under the table three women I knew who I was sure would be easier to love.

This relationship had been the highest and tightest wire I had ever tried to walk. It scared me and wore me out. But I'd promised a dozen times I wouldn't leave. She'd have to be the one to be strong enough to give me the sack. Not just for saying the wrong thing one more time. But for never quite being the woman she wanted me to be. She'd have to see there was no other way to stop our routine: her always hurting and me always feeling wrong. Generally, I was afraid of being alone. Afraid I'd disappear if there wasn't someone there for me. But for that moment, being alone looked kind of peaceful.

I was pretty sure she wouldn't leave me if I said I'd try to do better. She had an intensity that made my brain crackle and I didn't want to lose that. She saw the real wanting in my eyes then and her tough mouth softened a little. But as soon as she opened her heart a bit, the old disappointment flowed in. She frowned and asked, "Then why won't you make a commitment to me?"

I mimed a straightjacket with my arms around my neck and said, "I am committed to you."

I figured, if you keep them laughing, they can't get you. She was not amused. Her mouth pouted, exasperated.

She said, "I want you to make plans with me."

I said, "If this is the proposal I've always dreamed of, why does it sound so much like a threat?"

"Olivia," she said, drawing out my name so I'd know she was serious, "I'm through waiting for you. I feel like we're in a canoe paddling in opposite directions."

She was right about that when it came to making plans. The more she wanted me to move to a big city with her, the more I wanted to move as far from the city as I could. I'd started to think living at the ocean would set me free. And living in the city would kill me. Which both turned out to be true in a way.

But for the moment I wondered whether I should have saved the smallest fork for the pastries. And I hated Brooke's instinct for these proprieties. I played the sound of the ocean in my ears against my understanding that she had a novel and a half written and needed to make contacts to sell them. Myself, I was scared of city streets, I hated making contacts, and I didn't have any novels to sell. She wanted to rub fins with big fish, and I wasn't even sure I could swim on my own yet.

She'd always said it was the little things that first endeared you to each other that eventually drove you nuts: my jokes, the way she ate off my plate, her snap judgements, the holes in the knees of my blue jeans. Like how at first it had been wonderful that we both wrote. Then our careers, such as they were, began to play out our incompatibility. Lately, we'd both been doing a hell of a lot more live drama than writing anyway. But that's one of the joys of intimacy; there's always someone there to blame.

Maybe I was just taking a stand to force her to leave me. But I did have a desperate fear that I'd die never having started. I'd named that scene "Deathbed With Empty Desk Drawers" to humor myself out of it. Still, I felt like I was fighting for my life. I fortified myself with the sensation of wet salty air and said, "Brooke, I need a quiet place where I can do some writing."

She said, "We're two smart women. We could work that out. If you cared."

I said, "I do care."

21

I would never say Brooke hadn't tried. She'd argued, begged and cajoled. She'd applied her exceptional brain to every angle of the thing. I certainly wasn't always easy to love. And she probably gave me more last chances than anybody ought to. The bottom line always seemed to be her saying I didn't love her if I wouldn't do things her way. And me saying, who was she to tell me whether I loved her or not.

What she didn't know and I couldn't remember was this was the ninth time someone had asked me to move for his or her damned career, including seven times before I was ten.

All I knew was the topic exhausted me.

She'd said she was tired of waiting quite a few times before. But I didn't know how determined she was this time until she said, "As it is now, we don't have any future, Olivia."

I'd never had a future for as long as I could remember. I loved Brooke more than I'd ever loved anybody before. But it wasn't like I could just start having a future with her then and there without practice or anything. Maybe I could have started small, like planning a week or two ahead. But this moving was too big. I'd moved too many times and left too much behind. It was always like part of me died.

I shook my head. The way she flipped the cover on the matchbook in the glass ashtray, I half expected the last piece of damning evidence to turn up there — a confession signed in blood, a broken vow, a loveletter to another woman. But I was exhibit number one for the prosecution. We both knew I wasn't budging. Then she shrugged. She wasn't fighting back anymore. She wasn't even waiting.

I lost my balance when there was nothing left to push against. I started to think about waking up without her every morning for the rest of my life. That scared me. I wished I could unfocus her as easily as she could take those glasses off. I didn't want to see the vulnerable corners of her mouth or the way her fingers arched over her knife. If she was going to leave, I didn't want to feel it. What I did feel was cornered. As far as I could see I was either going to lose myself or lose her and I wasn't sure I could survive it either way. I shook my head, no, even though she'd stopped asking. I was surprised by the beaten snarl in my own voice when I told her I loved her.

She fixed her eyes on something behind me and said, "It's not enough."

The calmer she got, the madder I got. There I was gulping warm champagne to bury the urge to bolt. And she just tossed all the love I had to give right back in my face. I wanted to dash my glass and pound the question into the table, "Why isn't it ever enough?"

But she derailed the whole argument by reaching around the plates and glasses and taking my shaking hand in hers as if she were saying goodbye to it. She said, "I'm moving to San Francisco. You can stay or go with me."

By that time I'd drunk enough brandy and champagne that you'd have had to hit me with a sledgehammer to get my attention. So that's what she'd done. I held on to a shred of disbelief. It was a lot to swallow. But Brooke was not one to say things she didn't mean. We'd struggled so long I couldn't help but feel relieved. The promise of quiet was too inviting. The prospect of following her was too bitter. The loss, sinking as if the tide had gone out all at once, was too familiar. I put on a brave smile and hoped for the worst.

Then came a rush of nostalgia even before the last of the lost love was gone. Fingerprints on the silverware made me want to laugh. The linen under my forearm was as warm as my pounding heart. Hadn't this whole relationship run on the sensation of touching as deeply as we could while slipping through each other's fingers? If she was leaving, I could see I would have to pay attention, now, while I could. I didn't have to protect myself from her demands, because there weren't going to be any more. She shook her hair back and it struck me how strong and free she looked. And she knew it. I felt tons lighter and excited. And attracted to her. I thought, if I touch her now, I'll touch her more. And if I do that, I won't leave.

23

But her hand was already on mine. I banished my hesitation, turned my hand and caught her knuckle under my thumb. The old charge ran up my arm and exploded in my chest. I pinged my glass against the rim of hers and said, "Your adventure, dear."

I drank to that, another breakable vow, this time to let her go. She sipped. Her gaze lowered. She stroked my hand as if it were a shy animal. Her mouth relaxed and darkened and I could see it wanted very much to be kissed.

One more sip for me and tender heat pumped to the tips of my fingers and toes. All I could see was going home and falling impatiently into bed. How easy it would be to slip off Brooke's cashmere armor and hold her close. How nothing would matter anymore except to touch the familiar planes of her face, breasts, those muscled thighs. Run my tongue down the arch of her breastbone and her long thin belly to taste all the hurt and fear and anger and hope and regret blending into an afternoon of soft insistent sex.

I could see agreement in her eyes. I said, "Let's go." She nodded. I finished the last in my glass as we stood.

We walked home, arms around each other. Red-orange leaves pulsed in webs of branches as if they'd set the cool blue sky on fire. Considering the whining acceleration of my desire for her, I couldn't understand why I suddenly felt so langorous, slow and sleepy when we finally climbed into bed.

I hugged her and kissed her petal soft throat. But she had slipped far away. And everything else in the room had too, except the surface of the bed which seemed to be my only friend.

The shadow of the hanging vine moved on the wall so I couldn't help remembering the day, years ago, that Malcolm had gotten drunk and given away my puppy, Janis. How I'd gotten drunk then too and handed our houseplants to guests as they left, saying, "We've decided not to keep live things anymore."

I couldn't even begin to explain that to Brooke, so I dove

into the sheets instead, managing to murmur, "I'm so tired," as I sank.

The sting of Brooke's disappointment would have burned me if a wing hadn't already closed over me. Or a sleeve. Because there's a pale woman in a green dress who haunts the edges of my vision at times like that. I couldn't figure out if she was life or death or someone I used to know. But she would slip in and steal me away and chill everything. And no one else could see her because she was always there.

I rolled over and shrugged to the elephant plant stand. I half dreamed of Brooke's mother who was in a wheelchair when she lived. Now she stood in the kitchen where I had vegetables frying. She smiled and turned the pan over in the sink. I thought I was in the middle of something between them when I heard Brooke whisper, "Damn you," behind me and turn away.

CHAPTER TWO

By the first of November, I'd answered an ad for a caretaker's job in a cottage at the coast. I left before Brooke had a chance to leave me. At the end, when she unbolted the door to let me out, I saw her mouth unguarded and sad at the last. Then she smiled ironically and said, "Your adventure dear."

The connection between us sank its teeth in my chest. It left a warm pain I knew would dry up if I didn't keep moving. It was one of those damned if you don't, damned if you do things. She was such a funny one. She waved like a little girl losing her best friend. But I could feel her blue eyes then on my back, satisfied with how fatefully we move, like gears turning each other away.

I'd swallowed the hair of the dog that morning, the last of the white wine from her refrigerator. Then I fed my hangover paper cups of coffee to get it out of town. I found myself over the hill from the city, standing by the road, and I almost drowned in the fresh air. Excitement hummed in my knuckles. But, when it started to rain, my weak knees wanted to call a cab and go back, and give up casting off into the winter ocean gray. But I threw the thought under the wheels of the next car that swished by.

I had on a blue poncho, the color the sky would have been if I had been a luckier woman. From under the dripping folds, my outstretched thumb poured an anonymous benediction over the passing cars. I bet on an odd one to pick me up, wincing a little that there was no one there to take the other bet.

As I waited, every muscle I had knotted up against the change. I tried to slow my pulse in the cold, thinking I could suspend time until the catastrophe was over. My heart was a fist thrust deep in my pocket. I closed my eyes and let everything slip out of my mind except the gravel under my feet. But I opened them in time to see the green Buick pulling over. I ran and my joints warmed. Much as I missed Brooke, starting to move made me feel a heck of a lot better.

The driver had insurance salesman sideburns and, predictably, said, "Hey, you're a girl."

And if I'd thought I could get another ride in that downpour, I'd have excused myself when he started in on his hitchhiking reminiscences. It had been the high point of his dull life when some crazy man picked him up, took him speeding over a mountain pass, asked him to pull out the vodka from under the seat and be careful of the loaded pistol there. The romance of the road was a thrill to his weary bones. It was fast becoming soggy jeans and a thundering headache to me.

As I listened vaguely, he said, "This guy turns to me. He's doing seventy along this cliffside. And he never blinks his eyes. It's weird. He just looks at me and asks, 'Did you ever kill anyone you didn't hate?' "

27

I laughed politely and considered the madman's question while the windshield wipers cleared the scene over and over again. But I really only heard one word after that, like a baby's voice, incredulous, the first time she pushes the applesauce over the edge, "Gone?"

Spring and summer had slipped through my fingers. And several years I couldn't remember. And Brooke was gone. Or I was, which came to the same thing. Gone pounded on the roof of the car like the lead gray sky over the coastal mountains.

Plenty of times with Brooke, I'd stamped out the door wanting to smash the way things were. But I wouldn't really want to be gone. I'd freeze in the hallway not knowing what to do, overcome by the pattern in the carpet. Or I'd pace. And finally give up and knock. She'd never be surprised. Or I'd go someplace to cool off. And she'd come find me. But this time I'd slammed out in a big way. If I'd thought she would stop me · from leaving, I was wrong. She wasn't even going to be there to go back to. We crossed the county line.

I'd said so many times how I wanted a quiet place to listen to myself and write. When the way opened, I sort of had to go. Malcolm used to say he would kill himself someday because he'd said he was going to too often. "Eventually," he'd say, "There's nothing left but to do it." Which only goes to show, I could have talked myself into a far worse corner. But that wasn't a whole lot of comfort to me at the time.

My ride dropped me off at the Roadhouse in Floodport where the rain planked into coffee cans behind the bar. Colorless sound flowed from the TV in one corner. It was a little shack of a place, but the bartender huddled with a man in a khaki tackle vest at the other end of the bar and the emptiness loomed around me. I drank a couple of beers in smudgy glasses. glasses.

My jeans were soaked from the knees down. I considered my heavy pack and the mile I still had to walk to the beach. Outside the little window, the sky was water and the road was water and the edge of the world was melting under me. Tears splintered on the dune grass and soaked into the sand. The horizon, though I couldn't see it, was swallowing what was left of the sun. And it was hard to believe it was the same day that had started with waking up in Brooke's bed and asking the elephant plant stand why in hell I was leaving.

Above the ornate cash register a pink calendar girl straddled a sawhorse, almost unbalanced by her heavy breasts. I could see I wasn't going to be popping up to this place for a drink in the evenings. I remembered how I'd hung out in bars like this for years without a second thought. I'd assumed I was too tough or too innocent or too much like one of the guys to get hassled. Or I was hassled and never noticed it.

Then I remembered the first time I'd walked into a women's bar and seen lesbians in Emma Goldman t-shirts, and lesbians in trousers with rainbow colored suspenders, and lesbians with panama hats and carnations in their lapels, and lesbians in overalls, and lesbians with ink on their fingers, and lesbians with chalk on their pants, and lesbians in running shorts and tank tops showing off their biceps and breasts and thighs and sunburnt flesh, lesbians smoking pipes, and lesbians wearing astrological symbols around their necks, lesbians with long hair, lesbians with beards, lesbians dancing, lesbians pouring from pitchers of beer, lesbians discussing politics, and lesbians just sitting in chairs with their feet up being lesbians — how the scene had swayed toward me and looked so much like home. It had been like all the taverns of my life, only better. It had been so good to replace the pinup girls with Janis Joplin and Gertrude Stein. I was safe in the arms of my friends and lovers there. I guess it raised my expectations. And now the Roadhouse wasn't going to be good enough.

Floodport was just a cluster of buildings clinging to the old coast highway. Slow moving proprietors of shelves of dusty goods leaned on their counters and waited to serve the local loggers and residents of summer and retirement cottages. There was, of course, no gay bar. It struck me, as I watched the bartender wipe the tables clean, how this geographic circumstance could change my life. I stacked all the nights I'd spent in bars like empties along the wall. The time I could have now just because there was nowhere to go looked like a dry cave in a storm to me. I mean, it was shelter. But I wasn't sure who else I would find in there.

I looked at the calendar for the date this time, which verified my sense of a long night coming. It was only five on the Budweiser clock. But the snowcapped mountains pictured there set off another chill between my shoulder blades.

I'd been calculating the cost of a bottle of burgundy to warm me up in my unheated cabin. I was going to have to go in for food stamps the next day anyway. But I don't drink alone, I reminded myself. Everybody has rules. I could have been dead drunk more nights in a row than I could count. I might have forgotten where I went, who I met and what I did. But I never drank as much as Malcolm, I always made it to work on Monday, and I didn't drink alone.

For some reason that made me think of my mother after my dad left. You know the old story, she put him through college and he put her through hell. I could see her washing dishes and looking out the window at the weedy, fenced-in backyard. She'd be singing, "I Get Along Without You Very Well," soft and off-key and tired-sounding. And on the sill, there'd be a tumbler of pink wine. But she wasn't drinking alone. I was there.

As I settled up with the bartender, the image of Brooke and the shock of her name knifed into my already mushy heart. I could see her skinny in a blue workshirt and those steel-rimmed glasses, with a pale ale on the pub table in front of her and a dart board on the wall. She'd be philosophizing like she used to, about how everyone is essentially alone. I always argued that we were even more essentially connected. And we never could let the issue go, which seemed to me to prove my point. But that didn't really ease the pain of buying that bottle of burgundy.

30

I sloshed along the banked edge of the rutted road that flowed with mud. I couldn't read the numbers on the gray houses in the gray sand and the gray sky. I thought I would perish from lack of definition.

Eventually, I recognized the saltbox cottage the owners had described. It had been built by a displaced Nantucket ship's carpenter. The roof never leaked and the furniture was nailed to the wall. The rooms were rambling and cold. But everything I needed was there, including a view of the restlessly turning ocean.

I started a fire in the fireplace and then put my feet up on the desk, something I never would have done in Brooke's time. I drank burgundy from a chipped wineglass, swearing it was just this once. After all, I'd never spent much time alone. I sort of had to get over the hump. It scared me though, how little the world seemed to care that I had crossed that line. Such a little line in such a big world. The waves kept roaring. And I started wondering if I could let people come and go in my life like tides. Then I realized I didn't have much choice.

There were flannel sheets on the summer people's double bed. The woodsmoke smelled warm. But my sense of well-being was undercut by the sound of the toilet running all night. It seemed to be saying, down the drain, down the drain, down the drain.

The second night in the cabin, I dreamed of a man sitting at a table at the edge of a bluff. I could hear the ocean. There was a woman with no head. She wore a green dress. She gestured for me to sit down. But the man at the table was looking away. So I walked around to see him better. His head kept turning and all I could see was the neat hairline and the tan swatch of skin above his blue collar. My own voice said this could go on forever. I was shaken and then relieved to escape into morning in the cold empty room.

It was raining when I took my coffee to the desk and looked out the window. I found myself remembering Judith. Judith with her perfect sixties long straight black hair and her serious face like a difficult piece of music. Judith and her violin and razor blades and anisette and gentle boys. I was afraid she might always haunt me when I reach a lovely quiet place and start to write. Because when we were sixteen in Missoula in 1967 we put out an underground newspaper. And she used to take me to her parents' cabin and shut me up in her father's study to write. She'd cut and paste at the kitchen table, and bring me a toasted bagel and tea after an hour. After three hours she'd bring me anisette in a coke and we'd sit on the porch and watch the sunset light the canyon wall on fire. It was heaven in a lot of ways. The view was granite and pine there. But the way the wind in the trees rose and crashed sounded a lot like the ocean in Floodport. I wanted to nail my feet to the floor, because it scared me to go back to Leo's study, dark like polished wood, with its Navajo rugs and farmworker paintings, walnut desktop and window on the canyon.

All that morning the rain came down and the ocean came in. And piecing together what growing up with Judith had meant seemed the only way to keep from having to go through it again.

We loved each other as best friends, sisterless sisters, fellow intellectuals in some kind of exile. Nobody understood us as well as we understood each other. I was taller, flat-chested and blessed with a sinuous riot of brown hair I pulled back into a rubber band and tried to forget. The T-shirts and tight jeans that looked so nice on her round body left a roll of baby fat around the waistband on me. I was cheery and comic, the plain sidekick. She was the sad-eyed lady of the song. She was bright at math and science, and I had history and lit covered. We used to say, if we were just one person, we'd be brilliant. We felt as if we could dip into each other's minds, as if I could read a book and she would know what was in it. We used to say we'd raise a daughter who would blend our talents.

Judith always beat me at chess as if we were playing the same game over and over. She would practice her violin and I'd be amazed when her small dimpled hands lengthened precisely to reach a high note. There were times when Judith was too beautiful for me to look at.

Her parents, Leo and Barbara, were both college professors, well-to-do compared to me and Mom. They were Russian Jews with a heritage of craggy faces and the ability to read political weather as if lives depended on it. I liked that. Their house was a luxury of wide bookshelves, active discussions and good food. Sometimes I wished they were my parents. My mom and I had reached a compromise that mostly involved leaving each other alone while she watched TV in one room, and I smoked rollies and wrote existential poetry in the other. We'd been each other's mainstays for so long I wouldn't dare imagine anything else. Still, it warmed my heart when I'd catch Barbara crinkling her eyes in my direction as if counting me in as part of her fold or her troops. And Leo even told me once, since I didn't have a father, he hoped I'd ask him if I needed anything. I thought he was drunk; he had the proverbial fondness for whiskey. And I shrugged it off because I did have a father on the phone every Sunday and on my vacations for two weeks each year, even though he worked most of that time. Anyway, I couldn't think of anything Leo could give me except for taking me into his home and feeding me knishes and political strategies like he already had.

I was close to Judith's family, but I wasn't inside it. Looking back, I see there was a lot they never told me. Maybe they didn't even tell each other. You never think there might be secrets going on when everyone acts as if there aren't. But when I was sixteen, it seemed like anyone who was paying attention

33

was in pain most of the time, so I wasn't surprised the day Judith disappeared from a badminton class and I found her in the gunmetal gray locker room. She'd taken off her gymsuit and put on her skirt and blouse. She'd neatly turned one white poplin sleeve up twice and become absorbed in sawing across her wrist with a razor blade. There was no blood yet. Just a red raised welt. But she kept cutting infinitessimally deeper as if bowing the softest note you can hear. I felt sick but I put on what I thought was an ambulance driver's face out of Hemingway or Chandler and said, "Give me that." I might have been asking her to pass a joint.

She surrendered it equally impassively, though she was probably as scared underneath as I was. There seemed to be something on the floor she had to watch. I unlocked my locker and started to dress in case we might need to go somewhere. There were two more blades glinting on a kleenex on the bench. I kept my eye on them until I had a pocket to put them in. Then I sat down and stared at the floor with her, seeing only gray concrete. I said, "What is it?"

Her voice was dreamy. "I have to get away from them."

"Who?"

"My parents."

"What happened?" She wouldn't answer and she breathed as if she were at the bottom of an ocean. Classes were about to change, so I said, "Let's get out of here."

I hid her at my house. And, of course, that was the first place her father looked. He must have waited up for her. When he came to my door in the morning, he looked as if he'd been driving all night. My mom hung back in the kitchen, which usually I hated. But in this case I was glad.

Leo was a gawky man. When he sat on our sofa his knees were too high in front of him. I looked at the thick veins on the backs of his hands and remembered how kind he'd been to me. His hands were shaking even more than mine. But with the soft flesh of Judith's wrists at stake, I had to consider I might be

34

looking at the Dr. Jekyll side of something pretty scary.

He didn't ask me anything, so I didn't have to lie. He called me Livvy. Well, that was a family name only my mom or Judith ever used, so it made it hard for me to stay resolute. But it wasn't up to me to trust him or not. I just let him talk. He said, "If you know of any way to get a message to Judith, please tell her I love her. And I'm sorry and I want her to come home. And I'll do anything I need to do to work things out."

His bloodshot eyes didn't look as wise as they usually did. In fact, he looked like he was just this side of begging for help from me, a sixteen year old kid. He put his head on his hands. And I took a deep breath and said, "Excuse me a minute."

Judith was still kind of huddled among gum wrappers, Russian novels and cigarette papers in a corner of my bed. Come to think of it, we hadn't slept so well either. She listened to what he'd said like she listened to her violin to see if the notes were all right. She shrugged, still pretty much looking like a zombie. But when she got to the livingroom, Leo opened his big bear arms and she ran to him. They hugged with tears running down their red faces. He kept telling her he was going to make everything okay. He knew what he needed to do. I still never got what was wrong in the first place. But Judith looked resigned and relieved and more herself again. And they left thanking me and my mother, though I didn't see where either of us had really done anything those two couldn't have done for themselves. And it was a puzzle to me how one day my friend was ready to kill herself to get away from this man; and the next she was holding on to him like he was everything.

If I'd known at the time what I know now, I still never would have said I was in love with Judith. I didn't have the nerves hooked up to desire her. We were always together. And that was enough. Except two times when something else bled through.

We went to a wedding the summer we turned sixteen. Judith had a boyfriend named Doug. His father was remarrying. But in the morning I dreamed it was Judith and me walking down a tree-lined sidewalk hand in hand rehearsing vows. I woke up in a sweat telling myself that was too wrong a dream even to discuss. Then we got stoned and spent the day making dresses out of Indian bedspreads with broad blood purple and earth orange stripes.

Doug was the latest in a series of soft-mannered boys Judith attracted. She said they were harmless. They didn't touch her. We always sent them home early and slept together, by which I only mean sharing her bed. But still, who would you say she was really with?

Doug won at chess with Judith. But I forgave him that. I liked to hang around and watch her play, the way her hand rested on her chin as if she ultimately pulled her moves from the bone there. And I liked the Bob Dylan imitation Doug would do, balancing his half-smoked Pall Mall between his guitar strings while he sang "Just Like Tom Thumb Blues." He brought out a minstrel side of Judith. And she had a voice like a dip in a mountain stream.

Judith sat between us at the wedding, absorbed in the drama. The elbow I rested on the pew in back of her met Doug's elbow there like a brother. All I could see were the backs of Doug's father and stepmother and the Unitarian minister pouring red and white wine into a goblet.

I was pretty stoned and I wanted to whisper, "Their love is like a pink chablis." But the church was too quiet. And anyway, something about the ceremony brought tears puffing into my face. It was like I couldn't find my way out of one of those logic problems Judith always had to help me with. I knew how it felt to blend like that damned wine, but I couldn't let anyone know it, not even myself.

I realized if I started to cry, people would think the wedding had moved me, which would be such a hopeless misunderstanding, I had to put the program over my mouth to keep from laughing until the recessional had ended. Then no one would notice. Except of course Judith. We always laughed at things together. I whispered, "Just thinking unthinkable thoughts," which was the truth.

She nodded.

I avoided explaining or even remembering by developing a magic trick. I made glass after glass of the very good champagne disappear with a flip of my hand. After awhile there seemed to be something obscene in the formal flourish with which the tuxedoed caterer pressed a swallow of each fresh bubbling bottle toward me. So I liberated one from the cooler for myself and dragged it out onto the abandoned terrace.

I could hear Iron Butterfly on the stereo inside. The way the June sun bled into the foothills made my eyes fill. But I couldn't cry because there was nothing to cry about, so I danced wide-armed circles determined not to stop until I outran the fire in my belly.

Something broke. I leaned on the railing and my head pulsed like I'd been hiking up a steep climb. Something like love sang across the soft surface of my skin. But I forgot its name and the caterer's girlfriend arrived with clouds of light brown hair and puppy dog eyes. She picked up the pieces of cool green glass and spoke calmingly, saying, "It's good luck to break a bottle at a wedding. Each fragment means a year of happiness for the couple."

"Each fragment of what?" I cross-examined like a robbery victim gone mad. The girlfriend took a shard, gentle with the sharp edges, and held it to the sinking light. My stomach betrayed me and I had to run.

Judith found me in the bathtub sometime later. Beautiful Judith swaying among the blue tiles in the mirror with her black hair over her shoulders. Her eyes made me feel like I'd lost the chess game again. Why couldn't I ever figure out how to change it? I put my hand on the faucet and boosted myself up. Stepped out and smoothed down my bedspread dress.

37

She had caught the bouquet, but that wasn't why I felt like I was crashdiving out of a high flight. I collapsed to the edge of the tub and teetered somewhere between laughing and sobbing at the mess I'd made of myself.

She sat on the counter and said, "Livvy, I was going to call my mother to pick us up. But maybe I should wait until you're feeling better."

Her voice sounded so reasonable, but the idea was absurd. I chuckled and choked and said, "Heavens no. We can't keep her waiting that long."

In the year after Doug's father's wedding, Judith and I turned seventeen. Martin Luther King and Bobby Kennedy were shot. The Democrats dumped Lyndon Johnson. And Barbara and Leo hired me to tend bar at a series of fundraisers for antiwar delegates to the convention in Chicago. This, I thought, was an advance over the previous election when they dressed Judith and me up in straw hats and bunting to greet the current congressional hopeful. We were so far from cheesecake it had made us laugh. I was glad to have something more serious to do.

It was a time of basement rooms full of people. Judith and Doug would attract a circle of kids to sway and sing "Where Have All the Flowers Gone" again. Barbara would improve on her short stature by holding a petition on a clipboard over her head, and flashing with her dark eyes and brightly colored blouses the urgency of collecting signatures and votes. And Leo would be cornered by a strategy discussion of young men holding paper plates collapsing with hors d'oevres. He'd be listening the way I always saw Judith listening, for the music of the thing.

Whenever I unfolded the card table, flipped out the tablecloth and set up bottles of booze and mixers, Malcolm Williams would appear. Malcolm was a labor organizer friend of Leo and Barbara's. He was balding and barrel-chested and he always arrived on a beat-up old green three-speed bike, which he said was the safest thing to drive home drunk. I found myself looking forward to seeing his flushed leprechaun face. When he'd stay at the end of the party to help empty and wash glasses, there was something about the lacy line of soapsuds on his tan tennis arms that made me smile. He befriended me. He filled me in on the drinks I didn't know how to make yet. And the votes we were gathering for our peace plank — which always sounded to me like something you could walk across.

I had taken an obligatory look at the seventeen-year-old boys in Missoula and found them prick-driven and tongue-tied for the most part. And I wasn't about to look at girls. Unless it was Judith who was brilliant and beautiful and distant as a mirage. Malcolm was at least bright and kind and there.

He showed me how to pour even shots, but I invented my own system to create a constant stream of liquid over a constant length of time. I'd tap it out with my foot like music. And if I wanted to make the people fly, I'd hold the counting pouring moment like a final resolving chord. It was an intimate business, like sliding down the people's throats along with the tonic and making them shine; like I was the booze itself, the laughter, excitement, nerve center of the party, touch of confusion, gyroscope twirling.

Malcolm mixed me gibsons, which I drank for the little onion at the bottom. I was more hungry than thirsty, but I thought I had to take what was offered. And gin fascinated me. It was snake oil and Malcolm was the patent medicine man. It was smoke snaking out of a bottle and wrapping me and Malcolm and Judith and Doug and Leo and Barbara and the rest of them close together the way my heart expanded to embrace the whole sad world. And the smoke was hot summer evening haze and I could float on it. And there was snake oil pounding in my groin and I wondered if I was falling in love. Or just falling. And Malcolm looked so happy to be pouring me another drink. For a long time I thought he was devoted to me. And that was hard to resist. Now I think he was devoted to the stuff itself. But we were working together to make the party. We were partners. And it made me think: if any man, this man. Where the gin spilled on the linoleum floor, it turned into tiny snakes, tripping me up so I had to lean on Malcolm's warm shoulder a lot.

Two things happened at the end of the last party that made me feel like walking out onto the front steps and crying, shivering even in the clear summer night. There was the way Leo bent to pick up a paper cup and crumpled it in his big hand. Everything had wound down to slow motion and he looked everywhere for the trash can as if it were terribly important that he throw this cup away. My heart sank into laughlessness as he crossed the room without seeing the rest of the party litter under his feet. Maybe it's just knowing how things turned out that makes me remember him like a gentle old horse in the slaughterhouse unaware.

Then Malcolm told me a story about the only place in his career he couldn't organize at all, a brewery. Because management had a keg tapped free for the workers day and night, no one had cared if the wages were fair or the work was safe. He laughed bitterly. No one had wanted to change a thing. He emptied his glass looking funny and beaten, and he said, "I couldn't sign a soul."

If I felt safe with Malcolm, it was because even his bleary-eyed attention reassured me I was still there. I knew he was as lost in the snake oil as I was. So it wasn't for protection I huddled with him on the front steps while Judith and her family turned out the lights inside. He and the gin did keep me warm. And I admit I steadied myself with a handful of the hair on his chest. And I kissed him. Then I went in to sleep with Judith.

Until later that night I surfaced from seven leagues deep to Judith's voice saying, "No," as if to the dogs. I was confused. She had a firm hold on my hand. We hardly ever touched. But I remembered the soft sensation of my dream, and blood rushed to my face and I pulled my hand away from her. Apparently I'd stumbled through the fortifications around my heart and broken the rule of touch myself. I said, "Oh, God, Judith, I'm sorry."

She wrapped herself further into her father's cast off white shirt and rolled firmly away. She breathed like a person trying to calm herself down. I said to myself for the very first time: no more gibsons for you, my girl. And yet I knew gin was the one door I could bear to open. I stared at the gabled ceiling and the cold dew on the window and the shelves with Land of Oz books lined up beside mathematical treatises. I felt stranded at the edge of a cliff. If I fell asleep, I'd fall off. If I stayed awake, I'd go crazy.

I woke up alone in Judith's attic room. Everything I did felt like for the last time: taking my jeans and workshirt from the back of Judith's desk chair, making the bed, folding my nightshirt under the pillow on the left; the ritual of greeting the dogs, Judith's Weimeraners, who met me at the bottom step. They came in like a velvet tide and it broke my heart to push their wet noses away and let them lick my hands. I took my favorite cup out of the cupboard, the ugly violet one Judith had made in Art.

She was at the dining room table with what looked like the last pot of tea already set on a trivet, and the last pitcher of juice sweating on the oilcloth. She didn't say good morning, so I knew the axe was poised. While I poured for myself and memorized the jungle of plants surrounding the table, Judith shuffled a deck of cards. Floorboards creaked in her mother's study sounding to me like the shore I was condemned to sail away from.

I looked at the Hawaiian sunsets on the backs of the cards as Judith dealt. They didn't look inviting. But I picked them up anyway. And I said, "I'm sorry about last night."

And she said, "It's okay," again. And it still wasn't.

She sorted her cards and said, "What about Malcolm?"

I said, "What about him?"

41

She contemplated her play. "That's who you were thinking of last night, isn't it?"

Her tone was not exactly that of the confiding friend. Nor of the wronged wife. Though it had a bit of both of those. And a bit of blackmail, too. "Malcolm's sweet," she said, "And stable."

I remembered, on the contrary, how he'd called me his rock. But I picked up two sets of cards and said, "Two and three is five and five is ten."

She reviewed her cards and her strategy. "Two tens." She stacked her cards precisely and added, "It's good to have a man around to take care of you."

I didn't want to have a man take care of me. I didn't think. But she didn't want to hear what I wanted. She wanted to be reassured I wasn't in love with her. So I said, "I like Malcolm," which was true.

She said, "So why not?"

I said, "Why not what?" just to be contrary.

She said, "Last card. You count. I've got the rest."

I looked at my cards and said, "Just one for me."

Without looking up from writing the score, she said, "Why do you resist falling in love, Livvy? Why don't you just let yourself be happy?"

Part of me wanted to scream. Part of me thought she was right. For her it was so easy. Maybe Malcolm was a safe harbor for me. I shrugged and dealt. She said, "You know, a year from now I'll be gone."

Judith had applied to five out-of-state schools. She was planning to leave Missoula and me and not look back. That cut. I'd thought we were soulmates for life. But I was wrong. I dealt hard to keep from strangling her. She stared at her hands as if she couldn't feel them. She rapped the edges of her cards on the table like a guillotine, then fanned them open saying, "I hope you gave me some good ones this time, Liv."

42

From the outside, things looked pretty much the same after that. We still talked every day about school and politics and life in general. The connection between us unravelled so subtly I began to wonder if it had ever been there, which made me feel pretty crazy. Half to please Judith, I saw Malcolm more. Half to please myself, I saw her less.

My mother had an old tan sofa on its way to the Salvation Army. And the sofa had a rip that hung down in its black underlining. I stashed my caring for Judith there a parcel at a time and left it. So I could grow up and get out of there okay.

By the next spring, I was used to it. So, when the phone rang one Sunday while I was in the middle of the funnies, I wasn't surprised that, once again, it was Malcolm when it should have been her. And I didn't know what to do when he said, "Honey, Leo's shot himself."

I could see crocuses unfolding the purest inner purple on the lawn. I couldn't understand what these words could mean on a day with such a color in it. I felt like a rock climber stuck on a steep face, a familiar place I'd never been before. Malcolm's voice was like the climbing coach trying to stay calm and remind you where to put your right foot next. He said, "Can you go over?"

"Of course," I said. Nothing could be more important. But I no longer sensed that I belonged there. I wasn't part of the family anymore. Without a sense of irony, I asked him, "Does she want me?"

He gave me the right answer on a practical level to get me off the rock. "Call her and ask. Then call me back."

I despaired whether I could follow these simple obvious instructions. I'd have to tell her I'd heard what I couldn't believe I'd heard. But Malcolm made a wounded elk moan on the other end and I realized I couldn't keep him waiting while I fenced with eternity. So I said, "Okay."

And he let little sobs spurt like blood betwen the words as he told me he loved me and hung up so I wouldn't hear him cry.

That only made me feel lonelier, which wasn't a very good reason to call Judith under the circumstances. But it got me going.

Judith accepted my visit mechanically, like you accept food you know you need to live even though you can't make yourself care about it. They'd given her mother a shot to make her sleep. And there were a bunch of grownups upstairs waiting for something. The kitchen was stuffed with pans of lasagne and casseroles, since that was the only thing anybody could do about anything that day.

I took Judith down to the dining room and made her tea like she'd done for me so many times. She sat at the table with her elbows on the oilcloth and her chin on her dimpled knuckles. Her hair fell over her face as usual. My heart poured out to her, even the reserve I'd been hiding under the sofa. But I kept expecting Leo to walk into the kitchen and burst the bad dream.

She said he'd known what he was doing. He'd just paid up his insurance and her college fund. He woke her up to say goodbye, which she hadn't understood until later. He'd driven to their cabin in the canyon where things had been so peaceful for them. He meant, she said, for them to know it was okay. But he couldn't go inside. He couldn't stay. He was sick and he was going to die anyway.

I'd never thought suicide could be such a reasoned choice, but she said, yes it was. I remembered the last time I'd seen him at yet another antiwar meeting. How he'd sat in a folding chair grading papers as he listened. His blue-veined hands putting his glasses in his shirt pocket at the end. How he leaned over to ask me if I needed a ride home. I'd said I was with Malcolm. Leo had smiled and said, "Good." And that was it. Not much of a goodbye. But that's what there was.

I did not like the feeling people could just check out on you like that forever. It was scary. I started to cry. I liked Leo and I didn't want him to be gone. Judith wound up rubbing my shoulders and comforting me, which was hopelessly backward, but she wouldn't let me turn it back around. So I cried for her too. She told me it would all make sense eventually, which turns out to be truer than she could have known. But at the time, I felt like I'd have to die myself before I'd ever understand what all of this could mean.

We finished the pot of tea in a long silence with the sun throwing the leaded glass pattern from the window on the table between us. The old companionship haunted me almost pleasantly. She made a face like she would have at a bad homework assignment a year earlier. I could see the rituals of sympathy were going to be pure bother to her. I wished we could play hooky this time like we used to do when we'd hide by the creek behind the school and get high. That part made me feel giddy like I could almost giggle if it weren't the kind of time it was. I grinned a helpless grin for her. And then I saw she was going to be far away for a long time. If I hadn't already lost her I would have lost her then. By the time she returned to the living again, she'd be in another part of the country. I felt a little guilty because that hurt me more than Leo being gone. But I kissed her cheek and let myself out the kitchen door. The Weimeraners were licking her hands as I left.

The memorial service was in the chapel at the University which doubled as a lecture hall. There were absurd little notetaking surfaces tucked on hinges beside each chair as if Leo's last act were a lecture we would later be quizzed on. All I got out of it was the cold shower realization that life is a choice. There were speakers who made politics out of Leo's death. Which is exactly what he would have wanted. The family sat in the front row. Judith only looked in front of her. But I knew she knew I was there.

Malcolm wore a suit and no tie, which is also what Leo would have wanted. The poor guy looked as if he'd lost his twin brother and half of himself and couldn't find his way home. He held on to my hand for dear life, rubbing it like he was reassuring me, but that was okay.

45

He told me whiskey was traditional for grief. We went to his place and opened a bottle of Jack Daniels. I didn't like the way it fried my gut. From the pained look on Malcolm's face when he swallowed, I got the feeling he was trying to burn something out of himself, punish himself for being alive.

The sky was insistent blue outside Malcolm's window. I switched to plain soda feeling lucky to have a piece of this transient stuff, life. I was afraid, too, when I thought about it that way. I wanted to go to sleep and not see how close death comes.

The sun and the level of the Jack Daniels sank at the same rate. Malcolm told stories about Leo until he sank, too, onto the living room floor. All I could see in the hard hard world was taking his head on my lap and stroking his sweating temple. He smeared tears on my belly and said he wanted to die, he was afraid. I held him and rocked him, and his pain and my caring for it made a blood red circle around us. I wondered whether Malcolm was going to destroy himself like Leo had, he seemed so bereft. And admiring.

I added a shot of whiskey to my soda and let it warm my so slowly cooling veins. I coaxed Malcolm into bruise gentle lovemaking through the whiskey haze. Our hopelessness hung back for a time. I held him and we slept on the worn carpet until the whiskey wore off.

He sat up like he'd crash landed from another planet. And he looked bitter when he recognized me, like I'd stolen something from him. Then he said he was glad I was there and he kissed my head and I didn't know what to believe. He groaned and reached for the bottle in the middle of the floor.

Which reminded me of something Judith had told me that I hadn't understood. The word tasted like sterilized steel, but I said it anyway. "Leo was an alcoholic."

Malcolm laughed as if I was stupid. He said, "Welcome to the funny farm, Olivia. We all are."

I said, "That's what killed him. He couldn't stop drinking."

46

Malcolm said, "It's not the fall that kills, it's the sudden stop at the bottom."

He splashed two fingers into his glass and raised it in my direction, as if it was the whiskey that was keeping us alive.

Sunset in Floodport that night was drizzly and grim. But I put on my slicker and boots and went out anyway. It was the kind of time that cried for a glass of wine. But after thinking about Leo, I didn't want to be in the same room with that yearning. Even if I hadn't been alone.

I walked fiercely instead. The rain soaked into the sand so fast I felt like I was never going to have the energy to do what I'd come to do. Here I'd sat at the desk all day and had nothing to show for it but a blank piece of paper and a family of ghosts. I sat on a weathered log with wet wind against my face. Down in the surf I saw a sopping retriever wrestling with a branch against the tide. It made me laugh how that shivering mutt looked satisfied to me, having his teeth into something just a little too big for him to handle.

CHAPTER THREE

I dreamed Brooke and I were in a littered banquet room eating raisin cookies leftover from a wedding feast. An old woman in a gold sari asked us to carry a bowl of wine to another wedding. I started to follow her but the bowl disappeared in my hands.

I woke up laughing to myself in the ocean crashing silence. I padded into the kitchen, opened and closed the cabinet door. The sound of the catch rippled through the house. I noted the greening tips of the jar of sprouts by the sink with new interest. I'd run out of money the day before, but I had enough coffee and oatmeal and rice and beans to make it through the month. I could see I was going to have to give up drinking, except for special occasions, of which there were going to be damn few that winter. And maybe that was just as well. The thought gave me a strange ache.

My desk was too clean. I listened and waited for the tide to bring something onto the blank beach for me. The stories I was waiting for were like party noise when I was a kid and they'd sent me to bed upstairs where I could barely hear the sound of grownups laughing and talking and spilling things and singing old school songs. The muffled symphony would make me want to sneak downstairs to hear every word and nuance of the booming joketelling voices and the light brass fanfares of laughter. It felt like I'd never be old enough to stay up until the last coats were picked up off my parents' double bed and the last car door slammed. Certainly this gray morning by the shore I wasn't invited to the party.

I paced the room and walked the beach. Surely the world was full of characters. Couldn't I start a conversation with one or two? I'd watched people all my life. Why did I suddenly feel as if I had no idea how they worked?

Headlines on the newspapers stacked at the grocery up the road aggravated my alienation. The country had just elected Reagan with a booming mandate. I'd mailed in my absentee ballot. I felt like an absentee, too. From a home that wasn't there anymore, having just been covered by a landslide. I didn't know how to know if the "Moral Majority" or the military right was going to start picking us up. If that six-gun nut was going to drop the bomb, I wanted to be with somebody special to watch the end of the world. That made me start missing Brooke again, the only question left being, who are you going to run with when there's no place to run?

I stoked up the fire. Pushed a few more words across the desktop. Gave up and napped the rainy afternoon. Woke up having to remember where I was all over again. The rice and beans I cooked left me still hungry. I hugged myself under a wool blanket in front of the fire and let the longing that had been pursuing me overtake me, the ghost of an intimate touch. I swallowed the lack of it like ruby wine, warm in my throat and stomach. It reached my face and groin as the fingertips of a woman, a lover, Brooke. Rivulets of loss and loneliness drained from me and became roots reaching through the ground, thirsty for the ocean because it touched the shore that touched her. I held the thought of her soft skinny body, sweet curls. I even longed for the cut of her voice.

I returned to my desk and wrote to her. To say how I missed her. How sorry I was we'd come so far apart. I folded the letter and hesitated, looking out past my desk light reflected in the window to the wide ocean rolling in the night. I'd fought for this quiet place. And all I had to show for my first two weeks here was a letter to Brooke — the one I'd left in the first place to have the space to think for myself. But I was afraid alone. That's what I'd learned so far. If I started with Brooke, the spell would begin again. I'd write, she'd write, I'd need her more. I'd write my way back into her arms. And I'd lose this painful little homeplace I'd gained, my desk in the middle of nowhere. I was cold. I sealed the envelope and felt a little warmer.

Something was changing in those ocean gray days, the chemistry of my blood and bones, the shape of time around me. I dreamed of a woman in a green dress, abandoned, crying in the night, whistling under my window, knocking at my door. I woke with the sense she'd been watching me sleep, brushing my cheek with her fingertips. As I sat at my desk in the morning I felt her at my shoulder shaking her head. I wrote a couple of pages, hard won, like those pitiful yards of territory armies fight days to gain. Then I was restless and thirsty for something to celebrate and commiserate with. I eyed the clean halfway mark of the gin in the Beefeater's bottle. Decided this was nowhere near the occasion and started a long walk along the shore instead. But I heard the footfalls and crooning of the woman in green as she followed in the wind behind me. I walked faster. She wrapped her clammy fingers around my heart. I shuddered and turned. She popped behind a rock and left me alone. For awhile.

I'd never had trouble sleeping before, but some of those nights I'd find myself lying in the moonlight making up fairy tales about the shapes in the grain of the raw wood walls. One night I flat out felt like I was going to die if I let the fire go out before dawn. I couldn't talk myself out of it. So I put another log on, and, just for the hell of it, I opened the tattered canvas case of my mother's flute. My mother was a funny bird. I remembered finding her in the diner at Woolworth's the day my first Jr. High School band marched down Main Street with red stripes on our white pants. You could see she'd been crying and trying to pretend she wasn't. I found something sadly satisfying that night in the weight of the silver pieces as I lifted them from the case, from their bald red velvet lining. And I found something satisfying in the way they fit together.

All I knew were a few tunes. I'd only brought the flute to the ocean because I didn't have any other place to keep it and it was the only valuable thing I owned. Talented Judith had always told me I had a tin ear. But that night the wind swallowed my notes and there was no one but myself to please. The cold touch of silver against my mouth made me take a deep breath. And raise my head. Something released in me then. The night began to go a little easier.

Brooke wrote to say she missed me, too. She'd found an apartment with a view of the Bay. But she was afraid to walk in the streets at night. The city was a jewel and she was afraid to touch it. She said she sat by the window every night and wrote and drank brandy until she couldn't write and could sleep. She said, if I came, I'd know where to find her.

That made me want to give up the cabin, hitchhike to her damned city, wrap her in my arms and keep her from being afraid. We'd be safe in the streets together.

I was even safer where I was, I argued with myself. No one was going to mug me on the windswept beach. I didn't have to

51

lock the door. There wasn't much to steal. I was more afraid of myself than of anyone in Floodport. Myself and the cold. I touched my frayed pea coat on its peg and considered winter coming wetter and windier and darker. Then I thought of a warm bed in the city with steam heat and Brooke.

I wrote to say I would come, if she wanted me. I'd been right, you see, about one thing leading to another.

I walked along the bubbling surf and wondered if it was such a good idea. I was just beginning to glimpse the possibility of being all right alone. If I could survive this winter here I could probably do anything. For some reason I remembered being a little girl, almost asleep, and having my father carry me to bed. How I wished I could trust, relax and rest on the shoulder of life like that again. Wishing made me tired. Before I went to sleep that night, I almost wished Brooke would be too mad to take me back again.

She almost was. She wrote back in tentative handwriting. She had been to a coffeehouse palm reader who told her she would be unlucky at love. She wanted me to be the one to have the faith this time. She was wounded and cautious. It was going to be hard to win her back. But that was where the romance kicked in. That was something I could work with. I wrote visions of how we could do it right this time. I told her I'd quit drinking. I swore I'd stop slamming doors. I wrote long thoughtful letters to myself and addressed them to her. I made favorable omens out of everything the ocean and my dreams brought to shore, listened to seashells and heard her voice. I held on to the story of how we could be, as if it were a tree in a storm. I started to want to be with her more than anything in the world.

Then I wasn't alone anymore. As I went to bed in the cold sheets and looked at the ceiling, or woke up in the rosy gray day, or sat at my desk, or walked on the beach — I pictured her on the earthquakey avenues, or in the law school offices where she was working until her ship came in, or under the satin comforter in her bed in her stacked up box of an apartment. How she would smell of little cigars and Chloe. How she would read Eliot or listen to Mozart before she went to sleep. How she would be thinking of me.

The essence of our relationship was yearning. The less we had of each other the hungrier we were. It was impossible to resist. And impossible to be satisfied.

Maybe it has something to do with being born a woman, but all my life I've had this uncanny ability to know what people want to hear. And say it. Usually without thinking. I went to my mailbox one day and found one of Brooke's letters, her firm stroke through the return address of the law school, her tiny print adding her own street numbers below. I put my feet up on my desk to read, without surprise, that she wanted to know specifically how I thought this thing was going to work. Considering our history and the last fight we'd had, I knew she meant, is this going to be a monogamous relationship? I knew what the right answer was.

I'd had a running buddy, Flanner, back in Portland. She was an evening shift radio engineer who hit her stride in the wee hours and even then had more fantasies and beer going down than anything else. One night she met the girl of her dreams, someone who'd never been to a women's bar before and didn't think she'd be back. She wanted Flanner to call her. She offered to get a pen and write her number down, but Flanner grinned her this charming grin of hers and said, I'll remember it. Flanner was good with numbers. The next time I saw her she'd spent five dollars in dimes in the pay phone in the bar trying numbers she thought were close to the one she was supposed to remember. You could see her knocking her curly hungover head against the plastic wall of the phone booth. The more she couldn't reach her the more she was sure this woman had been It.

I looked out at my rainy beach and thought about Brooke, who was becoming more beautiful to me the longer we were apart. At least I had her number. I just didn't have a phone. Sitting where I was in the fearful quiet, monogamy started to look

53

like a fruitful country. Still, I looked out at the ocean and remembered those gut stirring old complications, women whose particular touches always got me in trouble. But what are you going to live for? I wanted Brooke so much by then. And I knew it wasn't going to be easy.

I thought of something she used to say when I was making love to her. I'd have my hand in her and she'd be moving and I'd be letting my weight down into her unfathomable softness, and she'd whisper, "Don't you want to possess me?" And I'd pause, though that was intolerable. I didn't really want to possess her. And be possessed. I'd want to stop and have a chat, define terms, negotiate. But her hips would be saying, "Don't stop," by then, and I'd see she was offering herself to me and I really had no choice. So I'd say, "Yes, yes, yes." And that's more or less what I wrote to her that day.

I didn't feel quite right after that. I walked in the rain and thought about rip tides. I felt like the guy who had to choose the lady or the tiger. Like there was no real difference in this case. It was love and be devoured or nothing. I didn't know any way to live but with those claws in my flesh. Not that Brooke was anything but a kind and well-intentioned woman. It's just the way we were together. Needing to have each other totally. Needing to be needed. Where would it stop?

You could say I didn't have to go back to Brooke. I could have stayed at the ocean and changed my life. But I had a fated feeling about Brooke and me and that damned city. Like I had to live it out, to find out. I called it being true to my heart, which was all I really believed in.

I made plans to get to San Francisco by Christmas, began to collect boxes again to pack for UPS. As my time at the ocean began to look short, stories started to come. Well, the beginnings of stories was all. Charming beginnings. Which seemed to be the theme of my life so far. I had no idea where the stories would take me.

By the end of the month I was having more good days than bad. One evening I looked at the feed and grain calendar and realized it was Thanksgiving. First I felt a pang as if I'd been travelling in space, so far from home that the old observances didn't make sense anymore. Then I smiled as I warmed up some rice and beans. I thought, hell, any other year I'd be stuffed with turkey and grog and groaning on the floor wishing I hadn't done it. This time I had a couple new pages I liked and a new ocean rolling peaceful feeling. I kind of wished I could send that back home for them to cut up on pie plates and serve for dessert. I drank tea to the health of Brooke and each of my parents and my old buddies in Portland who would be playing a foggy game of bridge by then. I slept a little better than the night before.

The next day was as low as that one was high. I watched the tide go out, taking all my fullness with it. The music and laughing voices were all too far away. The door downstairs was just a sewer lid leading to rats and garbage. Everyone was having a great time somewhere and I wasn't invited. I contemplated the fifth of Beefeaters again. I'd stuck it on the shelf over the refrigerator. My mom used to do that so I couldn't reach it until I grew tall enough to look it in the eye.

It brought me back to a night when I was nine years old and bored on a slush turning to ice New Year's Eve in Missoula, the year my father left and we moved to an apartment. We'd turned up the thermostat and I snuggled under an afghan to watch TV, where everyone in the world was dressed up in evening gowns and singing and dancing. My mom was in her blue bathrobe and pink nightgown and slippers, rubbing my shoulders with an absentminded touch, stopping now and then to sip her bourbon and coke. She was a sad kind of pretty but I don't think she knew it. I felt bad for her missing the party that night. I was nine years old and not smooth at all, but I wished I could take her waltzing across the dusty green screen. Someone was singing "Happy Days Are Here Again," real schmaltzy and my eyes were getting tired and Mom's were getting deep pink, and much as I wanted to watch the foil ball falling over Times Square, I could see I wasn't going to make it to midnight. So I asked her if we were going to have some champagne, which made her laugh a hurting laugh like she had broken glass in her throat. She brought me a blue liqueur glass with milk and a layer of creme de cacao, "Just for the New Year." I heard the clink of my glass against her fresh drink and smelled the sweet slightly spoiled chocolate taste, like the strong medicine smell of her drink that always stung my nose and scared me a little. I'd been cold like a star in the sky for a minute, then started to feel furry, and fell asleep warm on her lap thinking at least we'd made it special.

My instinct for the party was good, I thought, back in Floodport with the light draining from the November sky. I spread two glowing logs with the poker and set a cold one on top. Flames rose full of the ancient knowledge, how to find the feast hall where the colored banners fly. I knew the place where there was always more wine in the cellar and something to celebrate. And camaraderie, always someone to raise your glass with who would swear to be your friend for life before the night was out. Someone to buy another round. And someone to grab you by the belt and pull you back when you were hypnotized by the thin air at the edge of the cliff. Laughter and oh-so-spontaneous kisses. Once the party was started you never knew where it would end, but your hunger would be more than filled, your thirst would be drowned, and you could live lifetimes before it was time to go. Everyone joined in. Nothing was held back. And the clown would keep them laughing all night long, lose her shoes and wake up in some entirely unexpected place. It was like remembering a language I'd been forbidden to speak, and the whole sunken city that went with it. I brushed crumpled paper off my desk.

I mean, hell, I said to the empty refrigerator, if I'd had a bar here and some money, I'd have met some people who'd care that I was here. I'd have someone to be and somewhere to go, instead of pacing around here talking to myself and gazing out to sea like a madwoman.

The postcard I'd stuck to the refrigerator door answered me with the tipped wings of a seagull photographed against the red-orange setting sun. I'd been at the ocean long enough to know you never really see anything like that. It's just the pang of the artist's wish for freedom, strong wings, never having to touch down. Seagull life is not so easy. Even for seagulls. I didn't like the photo. It was an invitation to a wine and cheese opening that evening at the Hungry Puffin Gallery in town. None hungrier than I, I said to myself. And even though the card had come addressed to the summer people, I scattered the fire and pulled on my boots. I saluted Mr. Beefeater and left him guarding the family jewels.

I told myself I was starving for inspiration, but I was scavenging for more than that. I walked up the highway to town facing traffic that never came. A row of trees leaned out over my head toward the ocean, though the early evening air was heavy and still. The sun froze on the horizon beneath a blanket of drizzling cloud. It started to rain by the time I reached the bright blue storefront with the prematurely gray boardwalk running by. A girl's got to eat, I thought, as I pushed through the door and checked the driftwood clock on the wall because I seemed to be early. The only person there was the proprietress, a retired schoolteacher still in her church clothes. I hadn't talked to anyone for days, so I blinked like a mole blinded by aboveground light when she crossed the room toward me.

There was something of the soup kitchen in the way she shook my hand, me in my ragged rained on wool pants and sweater. I knew she would feed me if I listened to her sermon. I looked at the Ritz crackers and chunks of cheddar, on Wedgewood plates on a red checked tablecloth behind her. The shape of the red and white gallon jugs gave me a twinge, as if I'd recognized an ex-lover I hadn't expected to see. As I wondered if it was worth it, I saw it was too late to back out. And anyway, where else was there to go?

"I'm Jennifer Cooper." The woman greeted me with the authoritative grip of her dry hand.

I heard myself explaining my position with the summer people, graciously and reasonably, as if I hadn't been walking the floor, tearing my hair and examining the universe in exile for the past millenium.

"But what else do you do?" she asked, holding on like a terrier who has cornered an unfamiliar rodent and isn't sure whether it's a prize or not.

"I write stories," I said, knowing I should say: I try to write stories; or, I agonize, mostly, over not writing stories.

She said, "Ah," as if she knew then what to do with me. She stepped back like a door opening. "Would you like a glass of wine?"

I hesitated and told myself: you've got to stay now, sucker, you might as well have a glass. White wine, I thought, sits lighter at least. It tasted bad. So I smiled politely and drank more. The whole transaction was brackish. But I swallowed that too. Cheap wine. The more you drink the better it tastes.

Jennifer Cooper's prim smile looked just as distasteful. But she didn't press me to comment or buy her photos, which were garishly framed and all in the style of the one on my refrigerator. We had agreed not to blow each other's cover. She spent the rest of the evening introducing me to the tourists as "one of our local writers."

I stayed close to the table and stuffed my unspoken objections with crackers and wine. I must have opened up some, because several people with winter tans stopped to confess to me that they'd always wanted to write. Me, too, I thought. I'd nod them gracious permission to dream, or even to do it, if they liked feeling their sanity sucked out from under their feet. I'd never been romanticized before. I was surprised to find I didn't like it. One woman with a gold chain asked me didn't I find the coast inspiring? I smiled, "Of course," and waved her toward the seagull photos, thinking, it may inspire me to shoot myself before long.

Then a woman walked in who looked like I felt, disheveled and a little wide-eyed, startled when she looked my way. It was like one of those Marx brothers mirror routines as she approached me wearing army surplus wool pants and a dripping slicker. I scratched my head to see if she would do the same. She didn't.

She introduced herself and we agreed that we felt as if we'd met though we'd never been in the same place at the same time before. Her long black hair and rebellious chin reminded me of Judith. She was heavier and much more attached to the earth and no one else would have said the two were similar. But she did look like someone I would have known in high school. As if she'd washed out to the coast in the sixties and never washed back in again. She still had the earnestness I'd long since packed in a footlocker with my miniskirts and beads. Her name was Rachel and she lived at the other end of my street in a cottage belonging to her grandmother. Holing up and making music, she said. Music, I thought sadly, there's a whole other language I don't begin to understand.

Rachel was standoffish with the tourists. They were in her way as she sniffed at the photographs of stuffed seagulls as if they were overripe cheese. She circled the room and returned to shake her head without the least bit of discretion. It struck me that her gestures belonged in a larger landscape than Mrs. Cooper's gallery. If Rachel shrugged carelessly the walls would fall down and the tourists would crumble. She patted my arm as if we were buddies in the trenches. She said, "What a treat to find you here, though."

My heart swelled like a sleeping dragon. I'd been thinking the same thing, but it would have taken me months to say it. I was terrified to look into those blatant brown eyes. And afraid she'd leave if I didn't. I'm not usually shy, I thought. I poured myself another glass of wine, knowing it could make me feel as smooth as Fred Astaire. I gulped nervously, and she looked disappointed as if I'd run off in the middle of our conversation. I smiled to reassure her. And myself. Meeting people isn't so hard.

I offered her a glass and felt a little exposed when she said no. She smiled and looked into my eyes until she was sure I was paying attention. She tapped my glass and asked, "Do you do a lot of this?"

I wanted to put the glass down. It was glued to my hand. I said, "Not so much. Anymore."

She smiled again. She didn't look like she had ever considered not saying what she thought. "I was just wondering. . . ."

Her flower child face made her impertinence look sweet. And anyway, I liked her more than anyone I'd met in Floodport. So I said, "Wondering what?"

And she said, "Whether you control it, or it controls you."

I thought, good heavens, flower face or no, I've only just met this girl. Everyone I knew took it for granted, you drink, you get drunk. What else did God give us alcohol for? For a moment I could see that if you were ever going to ask this question, you might as well ask it first thing. I liked Rachel's bluntness. I laughed with a little despair remembering how I hadn't meant to drink. But why else was I there? I thought to myself: you're drunk, Olivia. It's too late to change the chemistry now. I had another sip. Rachel, with her milkmaid skin, just kept looking like she cared about me. Like something I hadn't seen for a long long time. She didn't even know me. And I was leaving town in a few weeks. So maybe it was safe to say, "That's a good question."

She nodded her raven head encouragingly, as if it didn't matter how I answered, just so we both knew the truth.

I looked at the last swallow of wine and wondered what it would say.

Rachel looked satisfied, as if I'd agreed to do something she'd been worried about. Just as I was keeping myself from saying, "Who the hell are you," she squeezed my arm and left me shaking my head in disbelief. I was angry. But I also felt as if she'd rocked me in a warm embrace. Then I noticed the last of the paying customers were leaving, and I finished my glass and stumbled into the cloudy night with them. Jennifer Cooper smiled like a grim peony and said, "Come again," as she shut the door firmly behind me.

My tailbone hurt at the sound of Mrs. Cooper's deadbolt turning. I was caught in the naked mechanism. Locked out and locked in. I knew how to find the party for sure. But did I know how to get home? I was like a spy. My mission was to get out with the secret information I'd discovered. I was a dangerous woman. I knew too much. My legs felt damaged. Fog blurred my way. I caught glimpses of something hiding behind trees. It was wet and windy and I felt sick but too scared to stop.

I could hear Malcolm's voice, his old joke, "We could always sell your mother's flute for whiskey." And Rachel's soft almost present voice, saying, "You wouldn't, would you?" And for a minute I was afraid I didn't know what the woman inside my skin would do. I wanted to shake myself and say, "You can't stop, can you."

Then I was angry at being scared. I pushed them away. Rachel in her dripping slicker, Mrs. Cooper in her spotless gray shirtwaist, Malcolm with his twisted grin. Wind roared in the trees that leaned out over the highway. The rain raised its voice and the ocean pounded steadily. I watched the foam race and curl. And my little life seemed far too short to be spending it this way.

I slammed into the cabin and found the Beefeaters by touch. I stalked down to the rocky cape. I thought fleetingly of jumping in the sea. And less fleetingly of finishing the bottle. You're drunk now, anyway, baby. I thought, if wine were a woman, she'd have betrayed me as many times as she led me on. And I took one shot, fire in my mouth, for courage to smash the bottle and the rest of its contents against the cliff wall. Glass flashed like a mirror breaking; like the window of the Hungry Puffin crashing, gin splashing wildly to eat at the edges of the phony seagulls' wings.

When I woke in the morning with my throat ripped open and my hair full of sand, the nauseous swamped sensation was exactly like waking up with a lover I couldn't tolerate anymore. Claustrophobic, like waking up in a coffin. Finding myself stuck, sworn into intimacy with someone who becomes uglier each day. But I was the only one in the bed this time.

That was the end of the affair. I finally recognized the woman in green. As I made up my mind to leave her, as I started to separate, I saw what had attracted me to her in the first place, the sensuous friend who would always hold me, comfort me. She was supposed to make me fly. And keep me warm. But it always ended like it had that night, me left with heavy arms and the weather crashing over me, the only protection being that I couldn't feel it. Waking up beaten and robbed when I had expected to be loved. She was the wraith in the waves who didn't believe I'd ever be anything but her lover. Because when she held me nothing else mattered. Before I even tried to get out of bed, I told myself I should have known better than to stay in such an abusive relationship. Then I laughed a little, in spite of my headache, to see I was all alone there, the abuser and the abused.

My throat was dry but I felt like I was out of the desert this time. Every depressed corpuscle in my cold body participated in a grin as I remembered the crash of glass against the cliff wall in the night. I'd seen what I was up against. I'd said it, hadn't I, to that woman at the gallery. Oh, god, not that I could ever face her again.

I crawled back under the covers again. Another funny thought struck me. How I'd come to the ocean in the winter thinking it the perfect setting for the great breakup. And it was. But not with Brooke.

I kicked the fire and started coffee water and thought, so this is the lover I came here to forget. How impossible when she turns up every time I go out. Or even when I stay in, aching like a phantom limb. A lot like a limb, too, for all she'd been so close I couldn't see her. Half the time I'd thought she was part of me. It made me shiver as if I'd been haunted.

But now she was out the door. I was home, such as it was. I was in control. I wanted the old ritual of burning the love-letters, or throwing mementoes out in the snow. But she'd never given me anything, really. So I sang all the drinking songs I'd learned since I was a kid into the fire. Threw up. Brushed my teeth. Took a shower. Curled up in a blanket in front of the hearth and wondered: if drunkenness is a woman in green, what does life without wine look like?

That made me think of Rachel, which I thought I'd better not. So I wrote a letter to Brooke about how fresh the mid-morning path of sunshine sparkled on the sea. How I was really going to stay quit this time. Without mentioning Rachel, I wrote that I'd come to see how dependent I'd become. I told her she'd be amazed at the clean start I was making.

The rest of the week I had plenty to think of besides the empty space above the refrigerator. But sometimes at night I'd hit that sense of life's meaninglessness like dead water you can't sail through until it draws in its breath and starts to move again. If I missed the bottle of Beefeaters then, I reminded myself that drinking never really eased that feeling. Not for long. Drinking only made the next day harder. And on a good day, who needs it? I told myself it was just like losing a bad lover. Time would ease the ache.

The last day of the month, my paycheck came from the summer people. I put my bus fare to San Francisco in the silver-ware drawer and bought groceries with the rest. I drank sparkling cider out of a champagne glass, which felt a little silly. But no one was watching. I put a rose in another wineglass and set it on the desk where my latest attempt at a story had fallen into silence.

I warmed up coffee and watched a smudgy sunset. I'd begun to imagine I was orbiting somewhere between Venus and Mars, so I was stunned when Rachel's face appeared at the window. She tapped.

I invited her in and poured her coffee. She ignored the summer people's sofa and sat on the rug in front of the fireplace just as I always did.

"I wrote a song," she said, "A round. Something simple."

This was all practically stated, as if she might have said, "I've been planting potatoes in rows of seven."

I said, "I'd like to hear it."

She said, "It needs some words." She smiled, "I thought you might help."

I blushed for the story stranded on my desk. Rachel smiled wider like a birdwatcher who has identified some particular lark by heart and then confirmed it by the book. She blew lightly across the surface of her coffee. Something in her definite brown eyes gave me the feeling I would always be catching up to her; that just as I'd thought my way to some conclusion, I'd find she'd started with that as a given. She did not look surprised, for example, when I said, "I'd be willing to try."

I must have been lost in her eyes because she broke my trance when she put a sheet of music in front of me. It looked like the hoofprints of a beserk creature. I said, "I can't read this." My mother's flute looked as if it were about to disagree. "Well, I can a little."

Rachel said, "Good."

I said, "I mean, if I know how its supposed to sound."

"I'll teach it to you," she said.

"Oh, no, really, I'm afraid I'm tone deaf." As far as I was concerned, music was something other people were equipped to do. No one had ever liked my voice. Except when we were all drunk and indiscriminate.

Rachel said, "That's just because you haven't learned. There's nothing to be afraid of."

I felt like a child being cajoled to take good medicine or try a new game. Why do you suppose they call it facing the music? I argued with myself. This is too hard. Rachel was waiting for me to say something. I said, "You sing it so I can hear how it goes."

She had a soft, full voice, slowly singing her tune, la-la-ing for the lack of lyrics. Even with my tin ear I coud begin to piece together how the climbing, falling, circling melody would work with other voices. It was so pretty I was afraid to touch it with my frog voice. But Rachel kept singing. It wasn't such a fragile song. She pointed to the music in my hand. And I began to recreate the meaning in the intervals on the staff and the markings that break down time. I remembered being a school kid in band, keeping in step, getting by with mechanics, afraid to begin to understand. It would be too big. Like the ocean. You couldn't hold on to it.

Then Rachel said, "Now you."

I felt like crying. I said, "I don't know. Music. Singing. It's all too mysterious."

She nodded as if she'd been there herself, though I couldn't imagine she had. "It is mysterious. But that doesn't mean you can't do it. Listen, it's just like anything. The main thing is to keep breathing."

I took a breath. But then I discovered my belly, which was fluttering over being so close to Rachel. I couldn't remember where to begin. Which sound of all the sounds in the universe? I breathed out again. I was in a sweat. The fire crackled. I wasn't going to be saved by an interruption. I didn't even have a phone to ring. It was just Rachel and me and the music. So I gave in and asked her to sing the first note for me. She did. And I tried to shape my mouth as she had and make the same sound. And she nodded, yes. And I took another laborious breath, focusing this time on singing the phrases as best I could, remembering what I'd heard and deciphering the symbols.

She clapped her hands and said, "Perfect."

I was suspicious. But then she suggested we sing it together, which was much easier, letting her start, me leaning into the strength of her voice.

She said, "Wonderful. Want to try it as a round?"

I gulped, but nodded.

She said, "You have to sort of concentrate on yourself and ignore what I'm doing. After a while, you can listen, if you can keep your center."

She started and I listened to her for the song and to myself to find my voice. I closed my eyes and balanced the song on the rising and falling of my breath. I lost it a couple of times, but managed to steady my purpose and sing around Rachel's voice singing around mine. Eventually, I was so caught up in it I forgot to think about stopping until Rachel finally made me laugh at the endlessness of it. I felt as if we'd been sitting there singing forever.

Then my face was red again. I said, "I don't think I've ever sung sober before."

Rachel's eyebrows lifted high over all that was yet to be tried. "Well, play around with it," she said. She stood and walked to the door. I followed her. She put her hand on my chest, and said, "Thanks." And was gone.

I stood there wishing I'd put my arms around her. But then I was glad I hadn't. I started to pace. I was still going back to Brooke. If I touched this woman everything would change. This was not a couple of drunks flirting and then pretending it had never happened. Rachel's direct gazes unsettled me. She liked me sober. That was serious. I already felt closer than anything I was used to. If I touched her I'd want to stay. Brooke would be gone with a vengeance. There'd be no going back. I'd have to learn a whole new language and get used to the music and the sea. And who would speak my language? This woman didn't look like she had any idea what it was like to be restless and rowdy and bad. Brooke and I had seen the worst of each other. There were no surprises to fear.

Anyway, I thought, as I pulled out my mother's flute and put it together, I hardly know this woman. We haven't exchanged a hundred words. What am I getting worked up about? The sky darkened and the fire glowed, and I sat there for a long time picking out the melody and listening for the words.

After a while a phrase suggested itself to me. And the shape of a lyric. And I spooked myself. I was afraid I'd get involved with this stuff and never get back to Brooke. I took apart the flute and turned on the lights and started packing boxes. At midnight I walked to the phonebooth up the road and called Brooke collect. In the morning, I left the key under the mat, put a letter to the summer people in the box, and walked into town to meet the southbound bus.

CHAPTER FOUR

I spent one of the longest ten minutes of my life that morning on the Greyhound, watching the sun rise outside the double paned window, over the cloud of gas and disinfectant fumes. The bus purred in front of the Floodport Exxon, and I received perpetual advice from the front of the bus to watch my step, then wavered in the narrow seat. The air vent under my elbow chilled half of me. I couldn't decipher the ocean's whisper. But wanting to take it with me reminded me of the homes I'd left when I was a kid, with my feet braced and my arms flailing. How I would always make a promise to the landscape as it slipped away. That I would come back. And I never did.

I took Rachel's music, creased and smoky, out of my back pocket. Only the seven numbers she'd written at the bottom made sense anymore. The engine flexed its muscles. The door stood ajar. I wanted to run off and put a quarter in the Exxon phone and call Rachel and ask her to talk me out of going. Then I thought of the playpals in those old moving days who would promise to hide me and not let me go. But always did. My only recourse had been to forget their names.

The door sealed us off. The ocean stopped applauding. A shot of pleasure ran up my spine as the tires kissed the pavement and we rolled out of Floodport's grasp. There had always been that to make up for the losses: cliffside glimpses of morning lit ocean going by. The sense that nothing can touch you once you pull out of the station. The local paper folded on the seat next to me might as well have been in another language, from another planet, I was so out of reach. I had hardly slept the night before, so, as my face melted into the scenery and my breath slowed, I curled into my seat the best I could and slept.

I dreamed of a cake with honey-rich frosting and squat, old-timey Marzipan figures on top. Malcolm with his hands folded on the cream tablecloth. I wanted to remind him to bite carefully because the cake has a coin, a ribbon and a ring inside. His bald, round face was set in the righteous expression he'd always used when we were fighting for something: the tenant's union, the peace tree, the women's center. But his face had lost the flame and hardened into a barely-restrained bulldog attack. I said, "You can't use that face on me." His mouth hardened and I recognized the scar on his lip where some redneck had hit him at the Fireman's Ball. I remembered holding my bandana over his mouth while someone drove and drove and drove until we found a hospital. That gave me a pang, as if we'd been partners for forever and I was just now turning away. But that had all happened years ago. I said, "Leave me alone." He said nothing. I tipped the table over. His face floated there with a century of sadness in his eyes. Blood rushed to my arms with my whole heart behind it in the old reflex of reaching to comfort him. I said to myself, that's how quickly it happens. If you start again now, you'll never stop.

I woke with my forehead against the cold bus window. He's right, I agreed. I do have to deal with him. I adjusted my seat, watched the pinetree roadside passing, and reconsidered Malcolm.

Malcolm was my first bite of the apple, my temptation, on the one hand, to jump trains, jump bail and laugh all night. And, on the other, to be more legitimate than I'd ever be again. When the union transferred him to Oregon in the spring of 1970, he asked, "Are you going to make an honest man of me?"

I asked, "Are you going to get me out of Missoula?"

So, we had a little hippy Quaker wedding, in silence weightier than Lohengrin, with Janis, the dog, prompting the vows. My father came from somewhere with a case of champagne and a pair of sterling spaghetti tongs. He and Malcolm toasted each other. My mother washed glasses and cried. My father left on the night flight as usual. Malcolm and I put our bicycles in a U-Haul, gave the dog a tranquilizer and drove the old Chevy to Portland wearing wide smiles from the pot cookies and dexedrine.

Malcolm started organizing. I found a job at a pub called Shakespeare's and started taking classes at State. I'd be pretty happy mornings at the wirespool kitchen table, with a second cup of coffee, writing a paper on social stratification in the novels of Elizabeth Gaskell. I could see the Fremont bridge from my window, arching through the gray, and the flags at the top pulled at my heartstrings so sweetly I wouldn't move for fear of breaking it.

But the better I felt, the more Malcolm seemed to founder. Once he disappeared for three days and came home exhausted and drunk saying he'd tried to hitchhike south and forget everything. Whatever everything was. Another time, we were skiing, and he spilled red wine from a bota bag down the front of his white sweater. First he laughed and laughed. Then he lay down in the snow and wouldn't move.

Sometimes I thought it was politics, and I wondered whether this marriage would have worked out better under a Democratic administration. When Watergate came out and the Nixon era ended, Malcolm gloated, but he wasn't any happier.

We patched along with walks in the park when the roses were blooming and the dog could run free; or midnights at the Jazz Corner with smoky blue music, garlic in the air and two drinks for the price of one; or Sunday mornings in bed with the crossword puzzle when it was cold outside and warm inside and nothing mattered so long as you knew the seven-letter title of a play by Racine beginning with P.

Then, one weekend, our third autumn in Portland, all the things happened that usually happened. And something more than the usual happened, too. I don't know if it was luck, grace, growing up, lust, or the little insight that turns the wheel, but something changed.

It started Friday evening as I was finishing my shift at Shakespeare's by mixing up our house special, the Puck's Cup. I'd developed a routine, pouring quarts of vodka, tequila and 151 rum into a five gallon thermos on a chair beside the back counter. The grog sloshed carmel colored inside the cavernous chrome lining. The fumes stung. A gallon of orange juice, a gallon of sour mix, a bright red stream of grenadine as I counted five-six-seven-eight and cut it off, leaving half the bottle for the next batch, proud of my intuition for filling and emptying. I scrubbed my hands and arms like a surgeon at the stainless steel sink behind the bar, then grabbed a long twist-handled spoon, circled back to the jug and plunged my arm in far enough to stir the grenadine up from the bottom. Then I circled again, rinsed the goosebumpy juice-booze film off, grabbed an almost fresh sponge, clamped the lid on the thermos and wiped it down. I flipped a glass under the spigot and approved the sticky red-orange mixture that spilled out. I gave the drink to Myrna, the waitress, who had just finished her shift and was cashing her tips. She smiled, wearily appreciative.

Myrna was lean, gray, rougey and cigarette hoarse. As I lit her Salem, I said, "Here comes Malcolm."

She nodded without turning and said what she said every night, "He's a prince." I knew that was true. But sometimes I had the strangest feeling he was interrupting my real life.

I watched him approach in his predictable Mao hat and blue windbreaker, walking briskly as if on some important business. He had a perpetual public smile behind the soft beard he'd started when we left Missoula. To Myrna I said, "I have to admit. I like being married. There's something sort of steady about it."

"Yeah, I know," she tapped her ash. "That's why I keep doing it."

Malcolm drew up and put his arm around Myrna's shoulder. He crinkled his eyes at me and asked how I was doing as he opened his wallet and unfolded a dollar on the bar. I told him I was fine and let my hand fall on top of a clean glass.

"Puck's Cup, no ice," he said, as if I didn't know. And he blew me a little kiss, though I wasn't entirely sure if it was for me or the drink. I poured him one from my fresh concoction. I scooped ice into a cup for myself, poured in a slightly long shot of Beefeaters since it was Friday, topped it with tonic and squeezed in a lime. I put the drink on the counter then came around the bar to meet it. I untied the thong that held my frizzy hair back. And I pulled off the Tuborg t-shirt I'd been wearing over a turtleneck. Malcolm and I both sighed at the same time, which made us laugh. Then he rubbed my shoulders for a minute. And I kissed his head.

"You two," Myrna said.

Malcolm's rugby-faced friend, Brad, turned up and started to put his hand down my pants when I hugged him hello. I nudged him with my knee and he stopped, but it put me on edge. Malcolm didn't seem to notice and the two punched each other's arms and joked for a while. Then we decided on a bottle of Johnny Walker Red and one of rhine wine, which I bought from the storeroom with my tips and discount. We picked up Brad's wife, Linda, from the hospital where she worked. She looked tired, just like I felt. But when we got home and she changed out of her nurse's uniform and into jeans, we all started to relax. A few more drinks helped this along.

We lounged around on the salvaged mattresses we called sofas and stretched our feet out on the Goodwill rag rug. We had orange crates for end tables and coffeetables and bookshelves. But we had a view of downtown lit up like a carnival below us. Linda talked about the doctors she worked with, who had a drug of the week they'd get excited about and give to everyone — no matter what their problem was. Malcolm and Brad talked some politics and football. I described how the manager at work had called all the bartenders together that day and told us about the new bar policy, not serving drunks. We all laughed at that. I poured another round. "Who else do we serve?" I kept asking. We all laughed and laughed.

Brad lit a joint and he and I passed it back and forth until we had campfire lungs and giggles leaking out from behind our desiccated eyes. Neither Malcolm nor Linda wanted any. Malcolm looked kind of hurt every time I took a hit. It was usually trouble when we got on different chemicals. But, then, it was usually bad when we were both drunk, too. So, how could you win?

I hid out in the kitchen, making coffee, contemplating the evolution of the American refrigerator, and wondering whether it was my turn to wash the floor. Then Malcolm came out and said I was using the wrong filters and it was going to take forever that way. I said I didn't know we had any of the big ones. He said, "Why don't you look, you dumb pothead."

That made me mad. I thought, if this is the guy who is supposed to love me more than anyone else ever will, I'm in trouble. I looked at his whiskey blasted face. "That," I said, "is the keg calling the pot crocked, don't you think?"

I started laughing because I couldn't remember how the saying really goes. I meant to push him like he and Brad push each other when they tell a joke, but he was screwed up, so he kind of stumbled against the wirespool table, which wobbled along with him. He gave me this injured bird look, and limped off. Brad came in and looked at the coffee dripping and laughed and said, "Listen, we've got to go anyway."

He started to put his arms around me, but I propelled him back into the livingroom in a friendly way. A hug would have been nice, but Brad looked more like a quick wrestle. Which must have been the theme of the night because by the time I got to the bedroom to see about the coats, Malcolm had cornered Linda there and she was pushing him and saying, "Cut it out."

So I jumped in and slapped him hard, your typical wronged wife move. But what really made me mad was that women couldn't visit my home without getting the munch put on them. It embarrassed me and made me feel really lonely.

Brad and Linda hurried off whispering blazes between them. And I curled up on the mattress in the living room, feeling emptier than the overturned wineglass on the floor. It was as if I'd just realized for the first time that I couldn't trust Malcolm, and I couldn't have any friends of my own without him walling me away from them in his world. And he wasn't even there with me either. He'd numb out his brains and his eyes would roll up, and it wouldn't seem like there was anybody home inside. He was a bastard and I was stuck, paralyzed. Life was a mess. I was casting off into hot tears and sleep at the same time when Malcolm lumbered out and said, "Please come to bed."

He sat beside me and I rolled over and put my head in his lap because I wanted to trust him. That really made my eyes fill. And my heart sank knowing I should know better. I said, "I just want you to be my friend."

He put his face beside mine and said, "I will."

He put my hand against his eyes so I could feel that he was crying and that just made me cry more. He whispered, "Don't leave me."

74

This gave me a really scared feeling like he'd caught me about to jump off a cliff or something. I put my arms around him and said, "I won't."

Saturday morning showed itself through the windows as one of the last sunny days of Autumn. I rolled over and hugged Malcolm without remembering why I felt like I was giving it one last try. I liked the softness of his belly, and the fuzzy gorilla feeling of the hair on his wide chest, and the nipples in the middle of his armor. I dodged his morning hardon by kissing his shoulder and getting up and getting dressed and suggesting we bicycle down to Saturday market for breakfast.

He shrugged and smiled as if I owed him one. But on the ride downtown with the wind in my hair and the sun on my face, I found myself wondering what the first leaf to break off the tree feels like falling free.

After hot crumpets with raspberry jam and strong coffee, I hit that peak where life looks sweet and everything is possible. We strolled the crowded aisles of pottery and leatherwork, dodged around some jugglers and streetsingers, then slipped into an oldtown bar for a morning beer. Down by the river we found a stretch of grass and sunshine. Malcolm waved at some of the bums. I don't think he knew them. But he's the kind of guy who will register all the bums to vote one day and get them to elect him alderman. Sometimes I still expect him to pop out of a doorway full of winos and say, "Remember me?"

Anyway, we followed the bums' example and found a warm spot to take a nap. I floated off on the river of grass and then into someplace forgotten safe underground. When I surfaced to daylight I felt like I'd been hibernating in Malcolm's life for years. He'd protected me while I hid my heart, the bear that was waking hungry. Sleeping beside me, he looked like someone from my past already. I touched his hand to wish him well and thank him for letting me disguise myself as his wife. It scared me to think of going on without him. A cloud wisped into the shape of a Matisse dancer as I mused over the economics of leaving. In his sleep he pulled me to his chest smiling for all the world like a boy with his teddy. My heart stopped pacing like it had no room to move. I could see that before I could leave him I was going to have to throw away a couple dozen blues records that kept running around in my head. Women singing about the need I had for his need for me. I lay my head on his shoulder, less afraid for a moment, and thought, okay, I'll stay. Just for a while.

A cloud passed and we shivered and stood up and brushed the grass off each other. We pushed our bikes to J&M Liquor, where we stopped every Saturday, bought three cases of the cheapest beer in town and stuffed them in our backpacks. It had always before seeemed somehow worth the difficulty. But, this time, when the clerk said, "You folks must really like this stuff," I wondered if I really did.

Still, we puffed home with our load of lager. We opened a couple and Malcolm started a pot of chili. The onions were frying that smell that makes you feel like you're home no matter where you are. Linda Ronstadt was on the stereo singing, "Love is a rose and you better not pick it."

I thought about Alison, from my Women's Poetry class, who was coming over to play cards. I cut the shortening into the flour and thought of the white skin on the insides of her wide forearms. I rolled out the biscuit dough thinking, the less you handle it the better.

Alison was a large woman whose favorite clothes were overalls. Like me she was a few years older than most of the college women, and the early gray stripes in her black hair made her a little more different. In class she would sit back and take the discussion in, then when it seemed about to run down, she'd quietly say something that pulled the different strands together at a new level, and then sit back again. And there was some-

76

thing about the way she sat back. Sensuous, but in a frame of reference that was new to me. Not the sensuousness women practice to fulfill men's fantasies. But taking pleasure just being in her own body. And her mind. A lot of my life I'd been afraid of enjoying myself too much. I liked it that she wasn't afraid. I liked to sit close to her. Though it gave me an uneasy feeling. And I tried not to think about her too much.

Nonsense, I told myself, pacing around the kitchen, trying to figure out what to do next. This is not a crush, for crying out loud. It's just feminism getting under our skins. I paused to stir the chili pot and something stirred in me. Innocent political excitement, I assured myself.

But as I cut the biscuits into rounds, I thought of the doodle. How one day in Poetry, I'd drawn a little fish in the margin of my notes. And Alison, whose arm was a hair's breadth from mine, had taken out her pencil and changed my fish into a mermaid with very frizzy hair. I'd laughed a little and the professor had raised her voice, lecturing on about Plath's ice figures. I'd drawn in a ship cutting water with the mermaid as its figurehead. Alison had pouted at it a little, which clouded my delight. But then she had chuckled, which made me feel so good it scared me. She had covered my notes with her arm and scribbled while I contemplated critical reactions to *Ariel*. Then Alison had trained her eyes to the front and pushed the drawing toward me. I gasped a little. She had added a big-breasted mermaid with a knife swimming along and cutting the first mermaid free. I'd laughed silently and weak-kneed, noting that I only had ten minutes to pull myself together before class ended and I would have to walk.

I spun a little extra honey into the butter and creamed it with a fork, wondering involuntarily whether Alison would like that. I tossed an extra jar of artichoke hearts into the salad and disarmed the alarm going off between my ears. So what if she's special to me, I asked myself. There's nothing necessarily queer about that.

But when the doorbell echoed and Alison was on the front step, hugging me with her big laugh of well-being, my rationalizations thinned and I felt like I could melt into her soft settled body. Time slowed down and I could have stayed there forever with her breasts against my belly, her head against my cheek. She nuzzled my shoulder with unabashed fondness. And I thought if I didn't move away I would fall down in the doorway and make love with her right then and there. And I wondered what I was going to do with Malcolm. But I let go and smiled and pretended none of that had entered my mind.

I ushered her in. She handed me a book, Adrienne Rich's *The Will to Change*. Inside, Alison had written, "To Olivia, who has the will to change." I blushed and got that dizzy feeling again. She hugged my waist in a sisterly way and said, "I mean, you won't always be tending bar, you know. You are going to write that Great American Feminist Novel." Did I look disappointed? Did she blush?

Fortunately, our neighbor, Michael, arrived as a fourth. He was a haggard philosophy grad student, who took hungrily to a beer and a discussion of the day's news with Malcolm. I offered a beer to Alison and she said, no, she didn't drink. And she smiled as if she were offering me a gift. I was surprised. I'd never seen anyone do that before. I said, how about juice, and she nodded as if it were the best champagne. I liked the way she watched as I moved around the kitchen. Her little smile. I thought, she likes me.

Malcolm had started to get that beery sarcasm in his voice when he cut in saying, "Ta da! This is a special night. This is the first time I've ever seen Olivia make orange juice."

I glared at him. But he was on his way to the soapbox. "I mean," he said. "I mean, she's an artist at taking all but the last sip and leaving this microscopic layer," he held up his thumb and fingers very close together and made a clown face trying to squint through them, "So I have to make the next pitcher."

Alison laughed, "I'm sure she's an artist at many things."

I felt hot. Malcolm said lasciviously, "She is, she is."

I slammed the pitcher on the counter so that a spray of juice flew out. Then I wiped it up. Malcolm said, "For a bartender, you're a tad fumble-fingered tonight, aren't you, darling?" He stuck the darling in like a knife. Then looked at Alison as if to say, "I wouldn't bother with her if I were you."

I told myself I was imagining all of this and ladled out the chili reminding myself to smile and announce it as Malcolm's specialty.

All through dinner Malcolm kept sucking in his gut, trying to gain control of the situation, his face getting redder and redder. Alison sat across the table, expansive like a mountain, relaxed. The ache I had to get close to her was like an exposed nerve. I covered it by clearing the table and getting out the cards.

I shuffled maniacally, trying to bring myself the handful of cards that would ease my heart. Malcolm picked up his and said, "Who dealt this abortion?" like he always did, but I heard the words for the first time. I could see Alison mentally putting him on probation. And I wanted to explain somehow that he wasn't as bad as he sounded. I watched his fingers probing for peanuts in the bowl of shells beside him, blindly like an elephant's trunk.

We were defending against a game contract and I trumped a trick. Malcolm cleared his throat. We weren't working well together. "We took that trick twice, partner," he said, angry out of proportion to my wasting his good king. There was an ocean of irony in his use of the word, partner. I supposed this was our usual bickering. But it suddenly sounded rancorous.

"Sorry, partner," I said. "I was asleep at the wheel." I felt that way, too, like a truckdriver on amphetamines, trying to stay on the road, while all the gravity in the world was pulling me into the peaceful fields beside me. But I kept my focus from drifting over to Alison, who sat behind a card table face anyway. I led the ace of diamonds, which stopped their game.

Malcolm showed a void. I picked up the trick and Alison smiled.

"It's a good thing she trumped your king. You never would have gotten the other trick." She laid her hand down, "The rest are mine."

Malcolm wrung the neck of the beer bottle in his hands.

We changed teams for the second rubber and I found playing with Alison full of unexpected chills. Like when I'd pick up a trick and she'd say proudly, "That's my partner." Or I'd lay down my supporting hand and she'd say, "Beautiful." And I'd be caught looking at her looking at me. Surely she meant the cards. But all I could see were her blue-gray-green eyes. I felt as if I'd been seeing her face all my life. Maybe it's not exactly queer, I thought. It's not like I'm falling in love with women in general. It's just this person who feels like she could be my soul mate and happens to be a woman. I stood up to make myself stop looking at her. I tried to pay attention to the Van Gogh poster that had hung on my wall for two years. But it didn't yield any new insight. I found myself standing behind her pretending to watch the cards, reminding myself to keep my hands to myself. But it was already too late. Without my permission my hands had already straightened her hair (which hadn't needed straightening). I tracked my hands like a spaceship following an experimental trajectory into unexplored space. As they approached her shoulders, I wondered if this was normal or crazy. I couldn't remember how friends behave. I'd never seen anything like this before. But my hands landed softly on the new planet. I wondered what her neck would be like to touch. I wondered how I could possibly be wondering this. Straining the limits of friendly touch and swearing to myself I would stop there, I felt her calm breathing. She finessed and Malcolm lost another king. And under my fingertips she was chortling lightly because we'd made our contract. Her laugh made me laugh and my laugh made me feel like I didn't care. I hugged her and brushed my lips across her cheek. I thought I would drown. So I made myself stop grinning and return to my seat.

Malcolm picked up his cards again and threw them down. "Damn," he said, "I've seen better hands than these on a thalidomide baby."

He looked at Alison as if challenging her to object. She said, "One no trump." She held the high cards. She won the bid, so I was dummy again. I lay my cards on the table and watched. I couldn't help noticing myself noticing every move she made. So I did the safe thing and went out in the kitchen to make coffee again. This time I used the proper filters. And I decided it was definitely Malcolm's turn to wash the floor. I remembered doing it hungover and pissed off after fighting over it the month before. And realizing then that I could never scrub hard enough to make Malcolm feel safe. And maybe he was right not to.

I felt bad about that, so I went back out to rub his shoulders as he played. But the more I rubbed the tighter they became. He wasn't going to let me touch him. He looked at me with bleary eyes and said, "I love you," more accusing and confused than giving. Alison looked at us with soft eyes, but unblinking. I thought she was wondering how long I was going to put up with Malcolm. I thought he was wondering, too. He held my hand against his chest as if I were his life-line. I kissed his sweating forehead and looked at her and wanted to cry.

I didn't want the game to end. But at least, when it did, I was able to hold Alison again under the cover of leavetaking. We kissed cheeks like sisters, but it gave me a floating feeling.

Until the door closed and it was just Malcolm and me again. He was stacking dishes in the kitchen and he said, "So, you've got a new girlfriend."

Well, yes, I thought, still floating. Maybe I do. Why deny it. Malcolm was my oldest friend, after all. I walked into the kitchen wondering how we could talk about this. Without turning, he said, "Maybe she'd like a three-way."

I sagged. Felt like throwing up. I said, "You're disgusting."

"I'm disgusting?" He turned with a flash flood of wrath and I saw his fist form. For Malcolm, the pacifist, this was not a

81

practiced act. Nor fast. Nor sure. I turned. And as I caught the blow on the side of my head, I thought, he really wants to smash my face. He hit the back of my head as I charged out of the kitchen, and he chased me onto the front lawn shouting, "Slut."

It was cold out there, a cloudless September midnight. I thought he'd wake people, but he stopped shouting and took a position in front of the door as if guarding the house from me. Whenever I approached he hissed, "Slut," again.

I shivered and sat on the steps of Michael's house next door. But Malcolm shouted again and harried me until I moved to the step of the next house down. He watched me like an angry hound and I put my head between my knees and curled up in a ball. He finally slammed back inside. And I held myself and wondered where I was going to go. I couldn't think. I lay down on the cement. I thought I heard a train in the distance but it must have been in my own throat because the porch light went on over my head and the woman who lived there stood in her door in a quilted robe with her arms folded. She asked, "Are you all right?"

I pulled myself to my feet and said, "Oh, yes, I'm fine. Thank you."

And I walked slowly back to my own door and knocked until Malcolm let me in.

Sunday morning I woke up under the Pendleton blanket alone and thought, good. My nose was cold. My lips were chapped. My head ached. I remembered Malcolm kissing my shoulder and whispering how sorry he was, what an ass he'd been. I kicked him away and huddled furiously back to sleep.

I located him by the sound of running water in the kitchen, the slosh and tap of careful dishwashing. Something chilled me about the stack of murder mysteries toppling beside the bed.

One was titled, *Prime Suspect*, because, when a man is murdered, his wife is considered the prime suspect. I thought, my god, they really expect us to destroy each other one way or another. I abruptly decided to return the whole pile to the library. And get out of this situation while we were both in one piece.

The floor was cold under my feet. I wrapped the blanket around me until I could shiver into a pair of worn cords and one of Malcolm's generous wool sweaters. It was raining outside the dormer window. I thought, well, it's not that I could actually murder him. But I can't pretend I'm keeping him alive anymore either.

This reminded me creepily of a day Malcolm had taken me out to a field in the country where there was a headstone for a miner who had been killed in a cave-in. They never even dug him out, Malcolm said. Just put up a monument that said he was a faithful worker. Then they let the land go to pasture so the only witnesses left were cows. This made Malcolm cry. But it wasn't for the miner. It was for himself. "No one should be dead and alone," he said.

At the time, of course, I'd been touched at what a tenderhearted fellow he was. But remembering, I thought, well, the sonofabitch. He doesn't mind being buried alive. He just wants me there with him.

And I have been, I thought, making myself breathe against the deadness in my head. I couldn't remember the last night I'd been sober. I thought back for a week and gave up. Then I spit out the taste in my mouth hating Malcolm's generous way of keeping everyone's glass filled.

I combed my long hair and washed my face, feeling like a stranger to the pink-rimmed brown eyes I found in the bathroom mirror. And I thought about something Brad had said as he'd handed me the joint the other night. He'd said, "Olivia is fine, of course. But Olivia stoned is great." My head hurt. I thought, what the hell does he get from having me stoned? My permission to piss off the porch?

83

That made me laugh a little because it was probably true. I plodded back to bed where Malcolm had left the *Oregonian*. I turned to the ads for studio apartments with the most lively feeling I'd had in my heart for months, Alison notwithstanding.

The smell of hot malt was in the air as I walked into the kitchen. The floor was filled with steaming quart bottles and Malcolm was siphoning homebrew from the stoneware vat on the counter. He capped one bottle while the next one filled.

I thought of the four cases already ripening and the malt warming in the oven to make a new batch on the bottom yeast of this one. It was vile stuff. But cheap. And it supported Malcolm's wonderful project of making every soul welcome. There was an element of optimism there, too. A man with 96 quarts of beer is a man who plans to stay alive and drinking. Even after all these years I'd never stopped looking forward to tasting each batch. One of these times, I kept thinking, the stuff will turn out good.

I sat on an upturned case and watched with a slight shock at the muddiness of the brew foaming into the bottle. I thought, dammit, he's taking it off early. Sometimes I don't think he even wants it to be good.

I cleared my throat and said, "It looks a little wild don't you think?"

I had cleaned up my share of the wild stuff, the bottles that hit the ceiling when you open them, if they don't explode in the closet first.

"I'll risk it," Malcolm said bitterly. He did not look up.

I watched the soft flesh of his hands moving over the siphon and the army green scaffolding of the capper. I'd made an appointment to see an apartment, but it suddenly didn't feel fair. I touched his arm and he stiffened. I said, "Listen, I've been thinking..."

He remained absorbed in the stream of must.

"...I almost think we could work this thing out, if we both — at least — cut down on drinking."

He set the siphon, still running, inside a fresh bottle and looked at me without trust. His eyes reminded me of the donkey that realizes he's never going to get that carrot.

Each of his words sank like a balloon tied to a lead weight. He said, "Don't ask me that."

I'd expected this but it still pissed me off. I said, "Doesn't it seem like we always fight when we're drunk?"

His laugh started to release tension then took on a mean edge that cranked it up again. He asked, "How can you tell? We're always drinking."

I said, "Well, dammit, we're always fighting too. I'm sick of it."

He said, "Cut the shit, Livvy. We don't fight because we drink. We fight so you have an excuse to turn away from me."

The hurt in his bloodshot eyes would have torn me if his purring snarl hadn't already twisted my gut. Fine, I thought. I didn't want to start again, anyway. What I wanted was to hiss like a bottle of wild brew: "That's funny, I thought I was drinking so I could face you."

Instead I said, "I'm sorry." And I bent my head because I really was sorry, until I made it out the door into the peaceful rain.

It was a relief in a lot of ways, leaving Malcolm and all those bottles behind. And I could clearly see it was as much Johnny Walker as Malcolm I'd been fighting with. What I couldn't see was how sister wine followed me out of that house like a puppy who was sure she belonged with me. For example, practically the first thing I did was get drunk enough to tell Alison I loved her and wanted her, and that was pretty drunk. I remember carrying four glasses of wine to the table, forgetting that she didn't drink, and finishing them myself. For a week afterward I was running into people who said, "You looked pretty high Tuesday night," and I couldn't even remember having seen them. But I didn't care. I was in first love and I was coming out. And I felt like I'd been cleaned out with explosives from my heart to my toenails. Even the rainy streets looked beautiful to me.

One night I sat on Alison's kitchen stool and laughed at the careful way she buffed the mushrooms for her salad. I had a wine bottle between my knees and I was wrestling with the cork. It released and threw my shoulders back and I found myself looking into Alison's violet gray eyes. And the wine and bread and salad and the soup on the back of the stove just had to wait while we held each other close in the middle of the kitchen and moved to something slow on the radio. I liked how Alison started it, shy a little but definite in each motion of opening buttons on my shirt until her face slid from my shoulder down the slope of my breast which by then was all heartbeat. I clicked loose the hooks on the overalls that covered her large breasts and belly. There was nothing to hide from touching as much electric velvet skin across skin as we liked for as long as we liked. This could have gone on all night if we could have stood it. Flesh and feeling moved in circles meshing and moving each other, pulses insisting and resisting and returning. And it didn't matter anymore what the music said. We moved down one another's thighs so close it was one motion. Hands free to take, give, take and give — there was no difference anymore. Dinner was cancelled; the kitchen help had gone mad. And the room was filled with eons of soft mandala tapestries. Because hadn't all that weaving always been about slow exploding, opening, endless, deep touching, holding love?

Then I drank wine and we ate, and I drank more wine and we told life stories. I wished for harpsichords, roses, champagne in a pewter bucket, all the signs of a perfect moment. By this time we were sitting against Alison's sofa, curled up in one another's arms. Alison whispered, "Do you think this makes us lesbians?"

And I traced the line of her spine to the fullness of her ass and wondered how I could have had so much sex with Malcolm and been touched so little. I felt like giggling at how I had always loved his softness. Softness? I had had no idea. I kissed Alison's temple and said, "I don't know what you call it, love, but every molecule in my body is turned around tonight." And I held her closer and added, "And it feels like coming home."

But, by midnight I was on my back, turning my face to Alison's deep blue carpet. I was laughing and crying over the beauty of the pale green paper globe of Alison's ceiling light. Alison was stroking my newly cropped hair and my burning face. And I was wrapping and rewrapping my arms around her. I couldn't keep my balance but I couldn't lie still. I ran my face along the incredibly smooth skin of Alison's neck. I said, "I'm afraid I'm pretty worthless."

I laughed and buried my head in the wheatfield warm center of Alison's calm. But then I fell back thinking, that's not so funny. I asked her, "Are you still going to love me if I'm too drunk to stand up?"

Alison nodded, "I'll just roll you to bed."

She's stubborn enough to do it, too, I thought. But there were changes I couldn't read in her eyes. I said, "No, I mean, really."

And then I was on the edge of a tide of nausea. And I felt like I had seen this scene before. Pale green light swaying around our shadows on the wall fascinated me and hurt my eyes. Squinting made me think of Malcolm's bloodshot eyes in his maudlin hours. I closed my eyes and said, "Forget it. I'm a drunk. You can say anything you need to to a drunk. It doesn't count. Let's talk about it in the morning. Or something."

By twilight we were on some frosty anonymous curve of highway. I'd been riding so long I got my directions mixed up and couldn't remember for a minute which way we were coming from and which way we were going. And I wasn't even sure it mattered. But then I caught hold of a picture of Brooke in the city, making herself dinner, smiling her crooked soft smile, knowing I was on my way. Love spurted in my heart and I wished I could come to Brooke with the freshness of that first time with Alison. It seemed like there was something I was supposed to remember — a way to recover that innocence. But I dozed off amidst bus smells thinking, fresh is not the word.

CHAPTER FIVE

I dreamed of two men fighting, a mass of flesh and limbs and sweat on a canvas floor. Brooke was in the audience and everyone was jumping up and down and cheering for her because she had money on one of the wrestlers and she was winning big. I was happy because she finally got lucky.

I opened my eyes on the dry hillsides speeding past the spattered window. How pale the bone bare blue sky was. The traffic picked up approaching San Francisco. The cityscape crept up the horizon out the front window of the bus, and my feet trembled, reminding me how I was afraid of earthquakes and of the people who like living on the shifting edge. I wondered how you know what to trust there. Practice, I guess. Just keep putting your foot down and see that the sidewalk stays steady. Most of the time.

It didn't take long to start riding my own adrenaline into the stream of cars and trucks. I wondered where everyone was going. Some place at the center where the vectors would meet and we'd all pack so close we'd merge?

Surely they weren't all mail-order brides like me. Coming home to Brooke even though I'd never been there before. Wondering whether we'd finally be kind to each other, my high-strung poetic friend and me. It was, as the song goes, just like starting over. I knew our history of touch would give us time. The familiarity of my hand on her hip, her cheek on my forehead. At least at first we'd find our way all right. I'd tell her I'd missed her. She'd hold me and tell me she'd wanted me to miss her. Like always.

I mean, I thought something had changed. It had been easier to be honest, writing to her from the rain-dashed North Coast. And what with riding since the morning before while everyone else slept, I felt like I'd been through some trial and emerged new. Just in time to enter the mouth of the monster, this city where the earth's heart beats so close to the surface. I was sure I could win the lady's sleeve. After all, it was her call I was answering. We still knew how to call each other.

I closed my eyes again for a last chance vision. I wanted to find a treehouse in the city, a spot of green tucked away. One is all I'd need to keep that Oregon ocean storm in my head and Brooke in my arms. Or Brooke at her wide new flea market desk and me stretched out on the bed writing with crazy sunlight weaving across us through the window. Foggy fairyland streets to climb down into and make our dancing way through at night.

My knees shook. Our lives drew together fast now after I'd fought it and lost it and tried to wander away. I guess I was betting on the wrestlers, too. It was hard to believe we could do it this time. But it was even harder not to. Hell, girl, I said to myself, what else are you going to do with your life? I was wanting her in all the damp creases. And there was no place to back down to anyway. The emerald skyline rushed toward me like the surface of a swimming pool from the high dive. Then it splashed around my ears and I was in it. Canyons of highrises and flocks of people crossing at streetlights and shaking the sleep out of their eyes.

When we first pulled into the bus station and I saw that mirrored hall row of Greyhound after Greyhound, each flashing a different telepathic destination on its forehead, I had a strange urge to jump back on the next one going north. But I thought that was just wedding jitters, something I get every time I change my life for someone else.

I shouldered my pack and surveyed my cramped muscles and empty pockets. I saluted the "watch your step" sign and disembarked. Brooke was nowhere in sight. And without her to navigate by I was about to get lost in the ocean of bus station drifters. I was moving slower than these duffel bag hustlers. In the hard-nosed sunny cold morning everything was at an odd angle. Once I corrected for that, I recognized Brooke by her long thin upright shape under a new black overcoat, cloche hat and a perm that smoothed out her outlaw curls. Her characteristic glasses were missing, and somewhere in this quicksilver climate, she'd caught sun on her face while I was still Northwest green with wet sand in my ears. And not sure I was going to make the transition. Especially when I saw that her eyes, which had been blue a month before in Portland, were violet now. She shook her head and smiled reassuringly, as if she'd seen me wondering whether she was the same woman. She put her arms out and I closed the distance for the reconciliation I'd come six hundred miles for. But I almost bumped her nose with my pack frame. So I blushed and laughed and took my pack off and took her in my arms again, keeping one eye on my pack to be sure nobody nabbed it in the confusion.

She looked nervous. My land legs were shaky. I smiled and said, "You look different."

She said, "Contacts. Do you like them?"

"Sure," I said, and hugged her again, closing my eyes uneasily. "You look good."

91

She did look good. But the change unsettled me even more than the night without sleep and the strange winter light. The fog, or something, had smoothed her features out. Maybe it was the power to be where she wanted to be that had released the chiselmark between her eyebrows. And she'd always envied violet eyes. Now she was becoming what she had always wanted to be. It was spooky. I shivered, thinking I was also becoming what she'd always wanted me to be. But that was too scary, so I reassured myself that the move was just throwing things out of balance.

We went home to the stucco building with the stray bulletholes in the windows, up the rickety elevator and into the little apartment with the Bay Bridge out one window and a brick wall out the other. I patted the elephant plant stand and noticed that its fern had grown. I took a hot bath. Brooke made coffee and buttered scones. I held her with the old confusion as to whose heart was beating where. She kissed my forehead and said, "Wait. I have something for us."

I watched her back disappearing into the kitchen, her shoulders stretched tight as the head of a drum. I heard the gunshot of a cork in the kitchen and Brooke's excited, "Oh my god."

I'd like to say I thought, as I ran, of all I'd begun to understand about drinking. But my reluctance was not that articulate. It was no match for the temptation to slake my thirst just this once. Most of all it was a reflex, when I saw her standing there over the sink with foam spewing down her hands, not to waste it, but to slip my arm around her and swing my mouth under the fountain.

It turned out to be hard living together, two such strong-minded women sharing such a small new space. But we never discussed

92

it because we thought, if we really loved each other, it wouldn't be hard. Neither of us liked to admit failures large or small. Though I did write in my journal, *It's a sleepwalking love affair. We bump up against our relationship like the edges of familiar furniture in a dark room. We don't make love with passion, but with relief that we still know our way around each other. Sometimes I wish we were still writing letters. Now that I'm here we've stopped opening our hearts to each other. The dream isn't coming true. And we can't stand it.*

Meanwhile, I hunted for a job as if it were a beast I could hang from its haunches and feed from for the winter. Brooke cut my hair so I could pursue my quarry all the more swiftly and silently. But this was a daunting task for any woman new in a city where steep crowded streets shimmer and threaten to shake. There were probably thousands of us with tired feet running out of money fast. What made it even more difficult was that the only work I'd ever done before was tend bar. And I was damned good at that. And loved it. And wanted to stop. It was like cutting off my legs and then trying to learn to walk.

Brooke urged me to find office work like she had. But I didn't type and didn't really want to and wasn't conversant with office culture. I didn't have the clothes. So, of course she loaned me hers. But they were never right and only added to how odd everything felt.

I tried the state employment service and a maze of beige personnel offices. After a week of this, I stopped one evening at a lesbian bar on Cole Street. And damn, how comfortable that dusky room with its glowing jukebox and clicking pinballs was. I sat on a stool and watched the bartender, a strawberry blonde with shortstop arms. After presenting myself at so many places that didn't need or want me, I itched to get behind the speedbar, scoop ice into glasses and show off. I missed those discerning drinkers who used to hang out just to admire how smoothly I poured colors and textures and flavors together. I felt like crying.

The shortstop worked her way through a couple of orders and asked me what she could get me. I'd meant to have a coke,

93

but instead I said, "I'm looking for work. I'm a bartender. You need anyone?"

She looked at me long enough to decide I was real, then answered as if it were a question she answered every day. "Not at the moment. But you can leave an app. Manager comes in after nine. You might call back and talk to her."

I walked down Haight reminding myself why I didn't need a job in a bar. I thought about going over it with Brooke and it suddenly struck me as funny that we hadn't been talking at all about how I wanted to quit drinking. I knew I'd put it in letters, but she'd never shown she'd ever heard it. I suppose it was hard to take me seriously when I was always saying I was going to do it.

A woman approached me on the sidewalk. She put out her hand to ask for change, but what she said sounded like a small animal crying. She reeked of whiskey and was walking around sick, with red eyes and snot caked around her nose. She had stringy blonde hair and a pekinese face. She carried a string bag with a half a loaf of Wonderbread spilling out of it. Support hose drooped down her swollen legs, and a skirt turned cock-eyed around her waist. A torn and oversized jacket hung on her skinny shoulders. She gave me a look as if she knew something about me and I had better pay her off or I'd wish I had. I felt like throwing up. And I got this funny idea that if she died before I quit drinking, I never would. It was a slow race. I gave her a dollar. We both walked on.

The rest of the way home I thought about how Brooke and I were out on the streets, too, emotionally. Panhandling, not sure where we were going to find shelter, so accustomed to being desperados. I felt like we could take control and change that, and dealing with our drinking had something to do with it. At least it was a place to start. I was angry with us both for not seeing what was happening. When it could make a difference for us. I determined to talk to Brooke that night.

She was at a meeting of her writer's group when I got home. So I flipped on John Fahey's Christmas carols, made myself a sandwich and started unpacking some of my boxes. I squeezed my clothes into Brooke's closet and drawers. Then I unpacked my desk stuff, the stories I'd been working on at the Coast. I apologized to them for my neglect and they forgave me like old friends who always know they'll get their time. They were still nothing but charming beginnings, except for one that was halfway to something. I laughed and hurt at how hard these fragments had come. I laid them out like pieces of a quilt. I could almost hear the ocean behind them. That reminded me to pull out Rachel's music, which I'd stashed in a drawer. Another charming beginning. I blushed and wondered why I could talk to this stranger about drinking and not to the woman I'm supposed to be building a life with.

Brooke's keys scraped in their sequence of locks and she whirled in cheerful and brusque, hanging up coat and scarf and hat. She kissed me and said, "I see you've begun an affair with my faithless desk."

I grinned. "Good meeting?"

"Um-hmm." She sat in her rocker with her mail and the paper. There were headlines about three Maryknoll nuns missing in El Salvador. I knew from experience that was going to make her feel particularly queer. So I flipped on the radio for something more cheerful. John Lennon was singing "Hey, Jude, don't be afraid. You were made to go out and get her." That strengthened my resolution to have a heart to heart with Brooke. I watched her serious face and remembered with a twinge that, in spite of how far we had wandered, it did make me happy to be with her. She was harshly beautiful, smart, a good-hearted woman. And I loved her.

As I mused, her face went white. She looked up at me like she was pleading for something and said, "My god, he's dead." For a split second I still thought it was the newspaper, then I focused on what the disc jockey was saying and understood why he was playing "Hey Jude."

". . .the 40-year-old Lennon was wearing a white T-shirt and dungaree jacket when he was shot as he and his wife, Yoko Ono, entered an archway..."

My knees ran so cold I knew I'd never warm them up. Brooke somnambulated across the floor and held me while she stared out the window like a widow. Lennon was on the radio singing weirdly to his own demise, "The dream is over." I held Brooke hard. I might be afraid of what was happening or not happening between us. But everything outside our world was scarier still. Right-wing politics and random violence, and now the death of our own righteous rock and roll youth. I blinked at the city lights. Then stood and walked Brooke back into the bedroom.

I tucked her under the quilt and pulled the shade over the brick backed window. I turned up the heat and lit all the candles in the room. In the kitchen I put the cut glass decanter of brandy and two snifters on a tray. Medicinal, you know. For gunshot, snakebite and shock. We'll finish what's in the house, I thought, and not buy any more. We'll talk about it later, I thought.

Meanwhile, he sang, "You say you want a revolution." And I poured liquid fire for the wake. The candle flames danced in the brandy. And I started to talk just to keep her from drifting off and freezing. I told her how I'd sold Beatle cards out of gum packages to the other girls in sixth grade. How my gay boyfriend and I had spent the night of the junior prom riding in the mountains listening to *Abbey Road*. Shea Stadium, I said. *The Ed Sullivan Show*. Getting high to *Sergeant Pepper*.

She smiled feebly. But she talked, too. She had snuck out of the convent to see *Hard Day's Night*. Honest to god, the only movie they'd let the postulants see was *Sound of Music*. And by the time Lennon had said the Beatles were more popular than Jesus, it made her feel less alone in her own growing apostasy. Once, travelling in Zurich with a boyfriend, she'd thought she was going crazy. But seeing *Yellow Submarine* dubbed in

French with German subtitles had made her less afraid of the madness. Nothing could be more absurd than that, she laughed painfully. And after a little quiet, she said, "He gave back the Order of the British Empire, you know. Imagine that, giving back the O.B.E."

The radio described people lined up outside the Dakota holding matches or lighters in the air or just their two fingers in the old peace sign. You could hear them singing "Give Peace A Chance."

Thank god, the brandy finally slowed our battering memories and our awareness of how relentlessly those years had already marched away from us. The radio kept playing him singing, "You might say that I'm a dreamer. But I'm not the only one." We drank a few more tears and drifted into a warm pool where we made love like ghosts. Then slept, because, although we'd been gunned down too, we were still going to have to get up in the morning.

Two days before Christmas, after I'd run out of confidence for the seventeenth time, a gay counselor in the Employment Service referred me to a man he knew in Personnel at University Hospital. When I told this blue-eyed brother I was willing to do anything, he referred me to the head nurse on the bone marrow transplant floor. She needed a ward clerk on short notice.

She spoke like a WAC recruiter and looked like one too. "This job isn't for just anyone," she said, disregarding the fact that she was desperate. "We have mostly leukemia and aplastic anemia cases. They go through a long demanding process here for a fifty-percent chance of surviving. How do you deal with being around pain and death?"

"I write," I said. Hoping I would.

"Good. We have a dedicated staff here handling the stresses the best way they know how. I'm proud to say none of my nurses has taken to drink over it. It can be easy to do that, I know."

I wanted to ask how she knew, but something told me to keep my mouth shut and look sensible.

She looked sensible back. "You're lacking experience, but I'm inclined to take a chance on you. I'll show you the floor and you can see how you feel about working there. I'll warn you that most of our patients are bald from the chemotherapy, some have swollen faces and unusual color from the medications and changes in their blood chemistry. Some are on respirators or have infections in their throat and mouth so they can't talk. A third of them are children. The average age of the leukemias is twenty-one."

I smiled and followed her. I put on my best brave calm and looked in a few doorways. I couldn't see much but I kept nodding my head. And then I met the ward clerk I would be replacing, a young black woman in blue surgery scrub pants and smock. She smiled, shook my hand and said, "It's a good job. You'll like it."

And all I could see was the uniform she was wearing and the fact that I would be able to get out of Brooke's clothes. The head nurse asked me if I could start the day after Christmas, and I said, yes, shook her hand and skipped home.

That night I dreamed of the dissipated woman in her green gown again. This time she spoke. "So, you think they're brave. You like that." Then the head nurse was showing me through the ward again. I could feel the patients watching me, wondering how I was going to handle it. Not because they needed me. But because I had something to gain if I could face them. We stopped in the recreation room where I was supposed to exercise one patient's leg. Her skin was greenish and her leg was so frail, I was afraid it would come off in my hand. But I did it. And I

98

could tell they were all happy because it was going to be okay for me.

My mood improved considerably, of course, once I had a job. The next task was to make Christmas. A lot of years I had just let Christmas ride, hidden from it or drunk through it. But it meant something to Brooke. And it seemed like it was my responsibility to make her happy. Which scared the bejesus out of me. But I thought I'd give it a try.

She surprised me with a tree. I've never had a box of decorations stashed away in the closet, so I'm amazed when someone else does. We spent one afternoon strolling past Macy's windows. The crowd seemed friendly, and I started to think San Francisco was going to work out for us.

I hocked my wedding ring to buy champagne and brandy for Christmas. Malcolm would have appreciated that. I hung a stocking for Brooke and stuffed it with tangerines, poetry and little cigars. I hid lox and bagels for breakfast in a bag in the refrigerator. And I wrapped up the album from this new singer, Ferron, who Brooke fancied.

Christmas Eve we spent at our local, a gay piano bar called The Mint, where we could sing corny lovesongs to each other. A few stingers and the cover of other carousing voices let me forget my tin ear and fantasize that I really could sing. Jenny, the barmaid, had worked there for a million years and took a shepherdess' interest in her flock. One of the barflies would call her "nurse" and tell her his I-V was out. This old bar joke struck me as not quite funny anymore. But the boys kept crooning about how romantic lesbians are. Wanted us to tell them how we stay that way. And we swayed together and got to thinking we really were as cute as all that. The old carols filled the night with fuzzy angels. And we went home and made love like children sledding on ice.

We woke up hungover and unwrapped ourselves like white elephants. We treated our aches with champagne and coffee and tentatively recovered our appetites.

Brooke gave me a brown sweater to go with my eyes, and a copy of Rich's *On Lies, Secrets and Silence.* Brooke was too smart not to have meant that exactly the way it sounded. How far we had come since I wooed her with *Dream of a Common Language* years before.

A depressive dose of Ferron on the turntable and the greasy deli paper leftover from breakfast and one more year that I didn't find whatever it was that I really wanted under the tree. I ate a half dozen candy canes and we held each other and watched the lights blink on and off in the green branches. We both smiled weakly rather than say, there's something wrong here.

She smoked a cigar. I picked up trash. Then my blood sugar went over a cliff and I had to lie down. She came in with her coat on, hat in hand, kissed me dryly and said, "I'm going for a walk."

I didn't want her to go. I had nothing to share but a nasty funk if she stayed. So I kept my mouth shut and squeezed out a couple of tears around the edge as soon as she couldn't see. The sound of the locks behind her set me free to let the pain in my throat expand and fill the room. Interstellar space couldn't have been lonelier or more disappointing than this place. I didn't even have the energy to pick up the phone.

The phone. I dragged into the kitchen for the last cup of cold coffee, ruffled through a drawer for that old piece of music, then came back to the bedroom and stared at the phone. It didn't move. I punched in Rachel's number. I hung up before it could ring. I took a deep breath. Like she had said, the important thing was to keep breathing. I punched it in again and held on for dear life.

"Rachel, it's Olivia Bell from the Hungry Puffin and all."

"Hey. Whatever happened to you?" She sounded real normal. Like I'd gone off for a hike and come back a couple of hours late.

I sweated. I wanted a place where I could tell the truth. "I was afraid."

"Oh." That seemed to make sense to her. Lightning didn't strike and the earth didn't open.

"I have a girlfriend."

"Oh." A trace of disappointment?

"I came to San Francisco."

A pause. Maybe a little angry now. "So?"

So? After all of that, what did I want? I sighed. Still breathing, I smiled sadly to myself

"So," I said. There was one thing I'd been able to say only to her. "You talked to me about my drinking. And I've been thinking about it. Not being able to control it. I try to quit and I can't. I can't seem to talk to anyone about it."

"What about your girlfriend?"

"We're having trouble talking."

She sighed. "It sounds like you need help. That's the way it is, you know."

I didn't know, but I nodded yes, which, of course, she couldn't see. My eyes were getting streaky. I don't like to ask for help.

She went on pragmatically. "I'll bet there are a few hundred AA groups in San Francisco. You've got a phone book there? Why don't you give them a try?"

I thought, oh shit. I've called six hundred miles to find out AA is in the San Francisco phone book? I could have figured that out. Anyway, I didn't want to sit around talking with a bunch of drunks. I didn't have a problem. Just a little difficulty. Hell with it. I'd work it out myself.

"Thanks," I said. "Why didn't I think of that?"

"You sound a little sarcastic, Olivia. I am trying to help. A lot of people quit drinking that way."

"I know. I'm just not good with groups."

"That may be part of the problem," she said.

I was getting tired of the problem. I asked, "How's the music?"

"Good, I'm working on something good. I haven't been able to finish those rounds, though. I kept hoping I'd hear from you and you'd come up with something."

I blushed. "I started to."

She said, "Well, go ahead and finish them if you like. How are your stories?"

"The same," I said, heart sinking.

She said, "It's good you've started talking about what's happening. Keep talking. I don't care who to. It's hard. But you can do it."

I was about to cry because it seemed too hard. I said, "I wish you were here." And immediately thought, oh yeah? How would that work out?

She said, "Well. You can always call. Or come back."

I was really going to cry now. Didn't she know you can't go back? What did she mean by that?

"It's good to hear your voice, Olivia. You know I think you're special. Merry Christmas."

Special? Sounds like a kid who's slow in school. From where I'd sunk to, "Merry Christmas," was about all I could say. I pulled it together enough, though, to add, "Thanks, Rachel. You're special, too." She rang off. Then I felt like I was out on a snowy night in the mountains. One of those moments when you could walk in any direction but it's chilly and peaceful just standing there first.

I curled up and slept until Brooke came back. She said hi, and I said hi. Then she clinked around in the kitchen for awhile. I felt like she was pretending I wasn't there. But when I smelled the onions and curry spices, I started to feel better.

She brought me a plate and we ate silently in bed. She looked at me a little sadly and I thought she was going to say, "This isn't working." And I considered saying it myself. Except the warm food in my stomach made me feel kind of happy in spite of myself.

"You and I need to get out and do something. Let's splurge and take a cab somewhere to go dancing."

I rallied a little to that. She called around to find a bar that was open on Christmas night. Peg's Place had the disco going for a handful of holiday orphans. We boogied tentatively. I was having trouble looking at her. I was kind of wishing she were Rachel. Fresh, direct, down-to-earth.

Where Rachel was substantial and practical, Brooke danced like a banshee in the wind. Hall and Oates sang, "Your Kiss Is On My List," and Brooke reached out to touch me as we danced. It was a brushing touch that waited for me to interpret and make a move. For some reason it irritated me. It felt like a trap. Whatever I did would be wrong. I knew she wanted to tempt me and hold me. But I could see she was dancing off some silent rage at the same time. Or was it me that was doing that?

It was all very confusing. I called time out and bought us a pitcher of beer. The satisfactions of a couple of drinks seemed reliable. We watched the other dancers. Then I hid in the bathroom and talked to the toilet for awhile. I cried a little because it was all too strange. It seemed like I was really with the wrong woman this time. And I couldn't go through with being her lover anymore. But I needed her. I didn't know what else to do.

I went back to the table as a slow dance came on. She stood up and put her arms around me and danced me out onto the floor. I held her too close to keep myself from pushing her away. The way her backbone stiffened made me angry. I squeezed harder, trying to melt my own resistance in her. My body was doing two opposite things at once and I couldn't breathe right. I got scared and put my face in her neck. But then I felt closed in and mad. Part of me knew none of this was Brooke's fault, but there she was, and I responded on an animal level. I bit her.

At first she held me closer, before we both realized it was more than an affectionate bite. She pushed me away, which was a relief. She said, "What the hell do you think you're doing, Olivia?"

I shrugged a little shrug I used to see Malcolm do. It means, what do you expect, I'm just a drunk. It chilled me to recognize it. But I didn't stop. Brooke grabbed her coat and walked out, of course. I started to follow her, then I remembered I didn't really want to. So I sat down and deliberately finished the pitcher while the punk dykes on the dance floor tried to figure out what to do with "Rocking Around the Christmas Tree."

CHAPTER SIX

Harry Houdini couldn't have done it better. With nothing in my pockets but an out-of-state drivers' license, I made it thirty blocks from Peg's, through the locked wrought iron gate and front door, the rickety elevator, two deadbolts and my own trail of clothes to turn up in Brooke's bed before dawn. Even though the answers were written on wax, chained in a box and flung to the bottom of the bay, I remembered where I was and who I was with, two ticks before the alarm clock rang. She wasn't speaking and I couldn't blame her. So I went into the kitchen and made a bowl of granola disappear. My knees were dissolving but I made them carry me out the door and toward the hospital for my first day of work.

In front of a drugstore on Haight, I saw a stack of *Chronicles,* and I bent down to steal one. Curled up in the doorway there was the bag lady who had panhandled me the week before. She smelled of urine and her face was gray, but she breathed peacefully with her hands wrapped in the old jacket that was half under her head and half around her shoulders. It reminded me of scary times when I'd been so stoned the sidewalk looked soft enough to sleep on. I tasted a little nausea under the toothpaste in my mouth. I skipped the newspaper, straightened up, stuck my hands in my pockets and walked on, wishing I knew how to whistle.

Warm behind a cafe window, a young woman in a red jacket sat at a table watching the door. The way she smiled when she saw her friend walk in made me wish I had someone waiting to meet me. The streetcar rumbled by on its lonely wires.

Up on 8W, Sally, the head nurse, nodded in approval of my clockwork arrrival. My head ached. She handed me the uniform that set me free. I grinned. She directed me to Personnel. I clasped my hands behind my back to keep myself from saluting as I left.

The receptionist in the avocado waiting room awarded me a stack of forms, which I worked my way through as the excitement wiped out the fog in my head.

Needing someone to contact in case of emergency, I fumbled in my book until I found an old address for Judith in Spain. She probably didn't even live there anymore, but I had to put something down to keep the authorities occupied. After all, Judith owed me one, wherever she was. And I knew Brooke was leaving me.

I stopped with a long inhalation when I came to the loyalty oath. God, I thought, what year is this? A line of conscientious objector ancestors peered over my shoulder gently considering what to advise. They'd been forced to mop hospital floors when they refused to register for the draft. Here I was hungry and facing the oath before I could even work up to the floor.

I looked at the connect-the-dots acoustic ceiling. I didn't even know what was in the Constitution they wanted me to swear to uphold. Imagine as I might, I was sure I wasn't going to use my position as a ward clerk to subvert the government. I shook my head at the crummy choices: exaggerating my already stretched thin loyalties, or going home to a home that was no home at all with no job as well. I must have sighed like a leaky balloon, because the woman in the chair facing mine leaned forward sympathetically.

She looked like it was her first day of work, too, every light brown hair trim and combed into place twice; slacks, blouse and blazer neatly pressed. From her scrubbed face, walking shoes and wide-legged posture, I thought she might be a dyke. She grinned when she saw me checking her out. Then I was sure. I grinned back.

In her lap she had a stack of papers identical to the one I'd been struggling with. She held up her copy of the loyalty oath. She had signed it, Kathleen Swift.

She said, "We need the jobs, girl. If we go to hell for lying to the bastards, let's hope that's the least of it."

She made me chuckle. I liked her. I remembered the yearning I'd felt earlier when I saw that woman back in the cafe smile at the opening door. I said, "Do you want to go to lunch, Kathleen Swift?"

The rest of the morning as I learned where to put the lab slips, specimens and x-ray reports, I wondered where I'd found the nerve to ask the stranger to meet me again. Ordinarily I'd be intimidated by her neatness and self-assurance. But she'd been friendly, too. And it made me happy to think maybe we both needed a buddy.

When the sun came out at noon, we met in the courtyard. Her brown bag had rice cakes, cheese and carrots. She told me her girlfriend had packed it. My bag yielded an orange and a leftover egg roll which I must have packed myself. Kathleen turned out to be an expatriate from North Carolina fled to the gay mecca. Back home, she'd been a printer until the chemicals wore her down. She'd been job hunting here for six months before she found this one as a secretary for a research doc. We both felt lucky to find work at the end of the year when the economy and everyone's spirits were sinking.

I found her politically aware and funny. She had a hard headed girl-reporter way of asking questions about how things work until she was satisfied that she had her story. She reminded me of an ocelot, cute, but sharp and quick, too.

When our lunch break was over I suggested a beer some day after work. Kathleen sighed and squinted at the cloud-wisped sky. She cocked her head, which I soon learned was a signal that she had something important to say. "I guess now is the time to tell you — I'm a recovering alcoholic."

I laughed nervously, and said, "A cup of tea then?"

She nodded doubtfully.

I heard myself saying, "Good for you, though. How long?"

"Six months," she said.

I didn't want to see the pain in that six months. I was envious, too, of the hard-won edge of pride.

I smiled and said, "That's great." But behind that I was longing to turn back. Catch a big bus out of there like with Rachel and the ocean. I was wondering what the hell you do with a sober friend, where you go, what you pour for each other, how you toast each other's health.

I wanted to strangle the friendship right there. It raised too many questions. But I was curious too. I saw my fingers pulling at blades of grass, and heard myself speaking almost calmly. "I'd like to know more about it. I've been thinking about my own. . . I think I drink too much."

Three broken stone pillars stood beside us in the hospital courtyard. I watched a red spider skitter up one. I said, "I'd like to understand what's happening."

She sighed. I bet she knew I was tempted to run. That was

one of the risks she took. She punched my arm gently because it was too sentimental a moment, knowing we were going to be pals.

For two weeks, Brooke came home and circled ads for new apartments. I'd try to talk her into giving it another try. She'd waver. Then she'd go back to circling ads.

Kathleen took me out for ice cream. She said chocolate was good for depression. She gave me two phone numbers, a lesbian counselor who was good with couples, and a woman who had an apartment for rent. She said, "Use either one or both." I got the feeling everything was going to be okay, one way or the other.

That night I came home to find Brooke in her rocker in her red satin dressing gown. She stared at the candle flame glinting in her brandy glass. Her lips were tight. Her silence was furious.

I went into the shrugging stage. I couldn't figure out what I'd done that was new. The elephant plant stand wasn't giving interviews. So I poured myself a glass, sat on the rug against Brooke's desk and let a sip burn down the back of my throat before I asked, "What is it?"

The furrow between Brooke's eyebrows deepened. She sighed. I hoped she would decide it wasn't worth going into again. She threw me the phone bill. I was baffled. I said, "I'll pay half, of course."

"And your call to Floodport? On Christmas?"

"Sure," I said, beginning to get the picture.

"Who is it?"

"Just a woman I met." Now the pattern was familiar.

"Must have been a pretty important woman to call her on Christmas."

"Not the way you mean it."

"You never told me you were seeing someone there. You

109

wrote to me about the perfect solitude and the quiet and all your pure longing for me. Don't you think there's something dishonest about this?"

"I didn't tell you because I was afraid you'd get upset."

"Damn right. Damn right I'd get upset."

She crossed the room and pulled out a desk drawer. She scooped letters out of it and threw a blizzard of them at me, shouting, "Bullshit."

I started picking up letters and shouted back, "Christ, Brooke, give me a break. Even in jail you get one call."

Brooke paced back to her chair, waving her arms and saying, "Stop making jokes, Olivia. You are never going to give me what I want, so just shut up."

On the last word, she threw her glass. I couldn't move. It shattered against the desk beside my ear. Shards fell on my shirtsleeves and jeans. The horror on Brooke's face echoed in my stomach. She made a gesture toward cleaning up the mess, hesitated and recognized it was irreparable. She put her hand over her face as if she had been hit and left the room with a deadly finality.

The next day I called the second number Kathleen had given me. As a result I lined up a nice tiny studio apartment in the Panhandle. Its strongest points were that it was clean and available; and the landlady, a friend of Kathleen's lover, could give me till the first of the month to raise the deposit.

Two weeks later Kathleen helped me move. I still had my boxes. Some of them I'd never unpacked.

I put out my old coffeepot and the cup that Judith had made in high school Art. My books by the bed in the order I wanted to read them. My journal and notes on the garage sale desk Kathleen had helped me find. It was a unique desk, with "I love Bill Gribble" scratched in the top by some schoolgirl. Or schoolboy.

Kathleen watched my pleasure with pleasure. But when she looked in the refrigerator, which was empty except for a sixpack of Rolling Rock and a bag of tortilla chips, she said, "Pitiful." So we went out for pizza.

I shadow boxed as we walked, excited and nervous about having my own place. A block from the Sausage Factory, Kathleen stopped walking and looked at her toes and then up at me. She said, "I want you not to drink when we're together."

I laughed, "Not at all? Not even one beer with the pizza?"

She punched her hands in her jacket. "Right."

I looked around for an exit, but there wasn't one. Just the streetcorner, the night and Kathleen. She said, "Don't you want to help?"

I shook my head back and forth. "Yeah, sure I do."

She said, "Doesn't it make it easier to communicate?"

I knew that. I knew how the talk gets fuzzy. But I'd always taken that for granted. And I didn't much like being told what to do. Especially when it meant changing. Even if it was something I wanted to do. I wasn't sure hanging out with Kathleen was going to be so fun.

She said, "I'm going to be there with you. I want you to be there with me."

I sighed. It was hard. She looked tough. This was definitely what she needed from me. I didn't see how I could turn her down. She was my best and only friend.

I watched people milling in and out of the Double Rainbow across the street. The night was getting colder and I was hungry. I shrugged and said, "Okay," real quietly.

She said, "Thanks."

When we arrived at the Sausage Factory, she opened the door for me, and I walked into the hot pizza smells. I didn't want to think how hard this was going to be.

We haggled over toppings and laughed. She ordered a Martinelli's and I followed suit, doubtful that it was going to satisfy. I watched her taste hers. She smiled. I tried it. It was not

111

the same. But it was cold and sweet. And the sparkling in the cider had nothing on the sparkling in Kathleen's eyes.

The next afternoon I called her at work. I said, "I just joined the union."

"Oh?" she said. "How did you decide that?"

"A beautiful woman walked up to the nurses' station and asked me if I wanted to join. What could I say?"

"My god, girl," Kathleen said, "Where do you get your politics?"

"I can think of worse ways to make decisions. Anyway, she's on her way to your office. I told her you and I would volunteer to design flyers. You do know how to design flyers, don't you?"

"Of course I do, but what do you know about it?"

"I know you, don't I? Solidarity forever, chum. I'll see you at lunch."

She said, "Okay, Olivia. But I hope we don't have to join a new committee every time your biological wing-wangs flutter."

So we both joined the union. And some evenings, when we'd be pasting up a flyer for the Affirmative Action committee or whatever, Kathleen would show up with bagels and cream cheese and I'd get a pleasant funny feeling I was back where I'd been in high school with Judith and the underground newspaper. But this time no anisette, gentle boys or razor blades.

Some mornings I would wake up and not recognize the sea green walls, the foam pad, my body curled up alone there. The familiar touch of my clothes was a joke compared to the blocks of barred windows and sidewalks choking a few straggling trees. I'd think, I never wanted this city, this is not what I came here for. I'd sit under sterile light copying orders from one chart to another in a language I didn't understand. I'd wonder, with

112

Brooke gone, how I was going to know myself. I was afraid a lot. But sometimes happy not to have to be something to somebody any more.

Everything had broken down for me. But at least I could rebuild it differently. Like any gay divorcee, I took night classes. I didn't like to stay home. It was so quiet there. But the professor for my short story class would say, "you have to listen to your own voice," or "you have to be willing to tell the whole truth." And I'd get the spooky feeling this self-improvement binge was going to have wider repercussions.

There was a massage instructor who would say, "working with the hands is good for the heart." One week I walked into the spring night after two hours of exchanging massage, feeling cleaner and more relaxed than I had in years. Then I found myself in Maud's with the superfluous weight of my habitual Heineken's in my hand. I looked at the green bottle. It had nothing to say for itself. I knew it wasn't going to make me feel better than I already felt.

I drank it, resignedly. I didn't want to look silly. And I didn't think I could afford to waste it. Though I wondered how I could afford to waste the massage. And I wondered what I was putting in all this bar time for anyway. Waiting for Princess Charming? I watched the women at the jukebox, pinball machines and pool table. I located my favorite by her long blonde hair, wearing sweat pants and hovering near the pool players. She had a flushed face and a knowing stance. I liked looking at her. We'd talked about the weather and the Giants and where we were from a couple of times. Not much of a high point for the hours I'd put in on that stool, but there it was.

She saw me and walked toward me with a goofy little stumble. I smiled warmly. She hugged me like a long lost friend, and I tried to ignore the stale whiskey and cigarette scent of her. She focused on me carefully and asked, "What was your name again?"

113

I made one up and she said, "Oh yeah," and patted my arm and wandered back to her game. I mourned my razed fantasy. I stared at the frosty green bottles nestled in the steep shaft of the cooler behind the bar. Though I felt like I could hide in a corner down there with them, I swore off bars instead.

But when a long Sunday afternoon came around and I didn't know what to do with myself, I went back to Maud's to stretch out the slow hours with a little beer and pool. At five, I tore myself away gently and caught a bus to Potrero for my aikido class.

As I got off the bus and walked over to York, there was a long moment of stillness with the evening sun hanging low and spilling gold over the row houses. I felt suspended in time. But in fact, I was late for class.

I hurried up the wooden warehouse stairs and bowed my head at the entrance to the loft. I'd developed all the reverence an irreverent woman can for the time and the place and the women I shared it with. Still I felt like Julie Andrews in *The Sound of Music* bustling into vespers late and disturbing my serious sisters.

I tiptoed to the dressing room while Penny and Joy and Verbana and Kitty and Sally and Linda and Estelle and Ruth and Marlene and Margie sat, each gathering herself silently, kneeling at the end of the red and yellow mat. I tried to pull on my white gi quickly and quietly. The drawstring on my pants stuck halfway up my hips. I whispered, "shit," and tugged at it. The ties inside the jacket fumbled in my fingertips. I made a clumsy knot of my belt. And the swish of my footsteps dogged me as I walked to the place that opened for me on the mat.

When I sat in seiza with my classmates everything sank. I could feel the others through the mat and the slow wave of breath around me. I opened my eyes to the window across the long white room. The sun rested behind the hill and the houses turned blue. I inhaled the breeze. We all bowed and class began.

114

We warmed up wordlessly. I stretched my arms, legs, fingers, toes, backbone, wrists and neck, hearing my body in a language of cracks, welcoming my wandering mind home. When we knelt again at the edge of the mat, I felt embarrassed to have come to class woozy. I remembered how tempted I'd been to stay at the bar for another game of pool. And I decided it was better to come woozy than not at all. But it's sloppy, I thought. And it looks as if I care less than I mean to. And it's hard to pay attention.

Margie was demonstrating. The long black skirts of her hakama followed the movements of her bare feet. Her pendulum braid accentuated her straight back.

"Wait until your uke is committed to her strike and then enter," she said. "It's hard because your natural reaction when you see her hand coming toward your face is this —" she put her arms in front of her head and turned her face away, squeezing her eyes shut and shrinking into her shoulders. "That's like saying, 'This can't be happening.' Don't do that. It is happening. Be aware of the attack. See what it is. Stay conscious."

I practiced facing attacks. But I'd blink every time. Even when I could force my eyes to stay open, my focus would blur. My eyes refused to see.

I took some falls. I liked the solid thwack of my body on the mat. I liked the clownishness of this. I delighted in knowing I could fall and I could roll back to my feet and do it again. That being down didn't mean being stuck there. I noticed I would close my eyes at the moment of the roll. I'd find myself on my feet confused at where I'd landed.

I breathed and sighed and took some more attacks. Pay attention, I told myself. Relax now. Smile. Accept these blows. They're gifts. Something to play with. Something you want to see. I breathed. I stood my ground. My ground stood me. I cried out at seeing the whole thing: the strike, the opening, the entry, the throw. I was fascinated. I invited another attack and did it again. The third time, I was overconfident. The shadow of

115

my partner's fist surprised me. I ducked. But by then I knew I wouldn't always have to.

I wiped my face with my sleeve and knelt on the mat again. Margie was talking.

"Take the attitude of practicing with a live blade. This is the attack. This is the sharp edge. If you don't pay attention, you are dead."

And I wondered what it would be like if every moment were a matter of life and death. And then I saw that it is. That every moment not paying attention is a moment dead.

I was suddenly very tired of running from the blade without even seeing its edge. I cursed the time lost ducking blows. And not even just real blows, but imagined blows and anticipated blows, too, a whole lifetime of ducking.

I could see how hard it was going to be. I could see that it was going to take a long time. But I swore I was going to learn to stay aware.

There was another technique to try. Attacks, blends, big circles, falls. I might have to practice forever. I might as well start now.

I knew it was all wrong as I saw myself doing it — stopping in at Scott's Pit for a short one on my way to a rally Saturday afternoon. I was early. And extra time had always made me nervous. But I knew I was going to have to learn what to do with it.

It all seemed so obvious, the bored looking woman in the leather vest putting a quarter in the pool table and saying, "play me one," in that smoky, slightly pleading voice.

I said, "Just one," when I meant to say no. And, although she was the better player, she scratched. I won. She racked up another and said, "I owe you a beer. Give me another chance."

So I broke and she came back with a pitcher. And I said, "I'm supposed to be at the Civic Center. There's a demonstration

116

for the children of Atlanta. You know the murders. It's hell down there for people now."

She turned away like she didn't want to hear about anyplace else we ought to be.

When I saw the bottom of the pitcher and the clock on the wall, I said, "Shit. I've got to go."

"But you're winning," she called after me in a voice that wanted to haunt me.

The rally was half over when I reached the corner where I said I'd meet Kathleen. I wished she wasn't so short as I cruised the crowd. I wished I wasn't so dumb.

When I found her I saw she'd been crying. I didn't know if it was for the children of Atlanta or me, but I said, "I'm sorry."

She said, "You sure are. You smell like a brewery."

She listened pointedly to the speakers. But she seemed to be fighting something inside her. I felt like crying. And not just for the children. The gospel choir started to sing, "He Sees the Sparrow Fall." Kathleen patted my back and said, "I'm glad you're here."

I squeezed her shoulder and said, "Me too."

After the demonstration, we drifted up to our favorite Vietnamese restaurant and settled on cushions in a bamboo curtain shaded corner. Kathleen was quiet through the curried crab. I looked at her stubborn cowlick and joked, "Really, I just stopped at Scott's for bus change, and this little woman with a big pool cue wouldn't let me go until I'd won three games."

Kathleen didn't smile. She poured tea for me and herself. She said, "I need you to be honest with me. You say you're full of support for me being sober. But then you come in like this making getting drunk sound like more fun than I think it really is."

I shrugged and thought a minute. "Maybe it isn't such a good time."

"Then why do it? And why, if it's so great that I'm sober, isn't it great for you?"

117

I didn't want to hear that question. Kathleen's small but certain jaw set. Mine quivered. I couldn't think of an answer. Her eyes were steady on mine and she said, "The truth is you drink too much. I don't feel like laughing at jokes about you getting hung up in bars. It's not funny anymore. You have work to do, girl. Stories to write. Rallies to go to. Friends to meet."

"All right," I said. "I'm sorry I was late."

Kathleen kept looking at me. I knew that wasn't the point. I said, "Hey, it's different for you. You have someone to go home to when I have the weekend to get through alone. The bar is my family, the place I can drop in and find someone to talk to. Or just watch the lesbian life go by."

She said, "That's what bothers me, Olivia. You have this image of yourself as some sad, broken dyke, sitting on a bar stool with the best of her life behind her. That's bullshit. You have a lot to stay sober for."

I couldn't see much through the tears welling in my eyes. I knew our friendship was coming down to the line. I wanted to stop Kathleen before she demanded something I couldn't do. But there was no way to change the subject. Kathleen was not backing down.

"There are people who love you, Liv. Me for one. That lonely routine just won't get it."

Kathleen sitting there telling me I didn't have to be lonely only made me feel lonelier than ever. And helpless. And scared, thinking, how could she love me when she sees I'm such a mess. I take such crummy care of myself and I don't even like myself very much. I had tears running down my face and I was sniffling and wishing I wasn't crying, but I couldn't stop.

And she touched my arm and said, "I want you to know you could quit drinking right now if you wanted to. I know it's hard. I could help."

There, she'd said it. I shook my head. I couldn't say I couldn't do it. But drinking seemed such a small part of my unhappiness. I pulled back and built up arguments, thinking maybe Kathleen's biased. Maybe she's projecting her problem onto me. Evangelic zeal. Alcoholic vampirism. Maybe she thinks I'm an alcoholic because she wants me to be like her.

Kathleen's eyes were steady on me. And loving too. I sighed and thought, maybe it takes one to know one.

I closed my eyes and tried to see the future with or without. Both were wide open passageways. I couldn't see anything in either one yet. I imagined a chilled glass of white wine so dry it slides down the throat like nothing. Then I imagined knowing I couldn't have it. I said, "I just can't see saying, 'never again.' "

My eyes still closed, I almost heard Kathleen's head shaking. She said, "You don't have to."

I opened my eyes. I didn't want to be cornered into a decision I wasn't ready for. I said, "Everything you say is true. I appreciate your honesty. I know you love me."

"But what are you going to do?" Kathleen asked.

"I'm going to cut down. Get off my ass." I laughed to water down the splash of anger.

Kathleen's gaze was not satisfied.

I said, "I cut down on coffee, didn't I?"

She said, "You don't have a problem with coffee, honey. And you do have a problem with alcohol."

I couldn't help grinning at Kathleen's doggedness. I'd always been glad to have her on my side. Just at the moment I wasn't sure which side my side was on.

I said, "Kathleen, I have to choose my own time. Believe me, I'll be thinking about it."

She walked me up Haight where the Saturday night crowd was banging car horns and shouting. An ambulance had pulled onto the sidewalk and two men were loading an unconscious bag lady onto a stretcher. I recognized her stringy blonde hair and her drooping pink stockings. I shivered even though the night was warm.

When we got to my corner, I hugged Kathleen harder than ever and said, "Thanks, pal."

At the bottom of my dream that night there was a woman in a long gown singing. She had lines from hard times on her face. She finished a throaty blues song, and a few of us sitting at small round tables applauded. Smoke hung in the room. A tall young man who had been her lover stood up and embraced her for a long time then sat down again sadly. An angry woman came up to the singer and tried to pound her with her fists, tried to scratch her. But she couldn't. The singer put her hands on the woman's face and said, "This doesn't mean we won't meet again."

I woke up really uneasy. As if I'd forgotten something vital, taken a wrong turn. Time was hurrying, flickering like speeded up film, taking me further in the wrong direction. I'd forgotten to pay attention.

I took a deep breath. And another. And time slowed down to one moment at a time. Did I know what to do with it?

I touched my face. Flung the sheet back and looked at my body, gray in the dawn and softened by the kneading of gravity. How could I be almost thirty and not remember living those years?

The room sparkled and I realized it was from warm tears. At least I was still alive. And there was something I was supposed to decide.

I remembered what it was and got up off my bed resolutely. I dressed in a shirt, jeans and a sweater, as if for battle. I found an apple on top of the refrigerator and bit into it. My stomach greeted the food appreciatively. I took another breath and walked out the door.

The Panhandle was spring green. Eucalyptus pods crunched under my feet. In the park the rhodies were blossoming relentlessly. I walked past the conservatory and the amphitheater. Congas conversed in the sunshine.

I thought about Alison and what she'd said and what she hadn't said one early spring Sunday afternoon years before. We'd started off to watch a softball game and I'd grabbed her arm to duck into Shakespeare's for a sixpack. While I waited for the bartender to make change, I stroked Alison's elf silk hair. I loved her so much. On the jukebox, Tenille was singing, "I never wanted to touch a man the way I want to touch you."

Alison said, "You know, Olivia, we don't have to take beer with us everywhere we go."

I saw love and weary righteousness in her color-changing eyes. I said, "What are you getting at? Do I drink too much?"

She shrugged, quietly angry. She started working evenings at a battered women's shelter. I started hanging out at the Rising Moon. I hated to be home alone. So, a good night was when I'd see her blue Pendleton coat on the living room chair and know she'd gotten there first. Whenever I went to bed smelling of the bar, she'd turn her back. But we didn't figure out any other way to do it. Until we were too far apart to come back together. And I couldn't understand for the longest time how I'd lost her.

I wandered down a horse trail in Golden Gate Park five years later and wanted to ask her, "Alison, do I drink too much?"

Not like I didn't know. Not like people hadn't told me. It had been so easy not to hear. But I remembered. There had been another spring Sunday afternoon, a bunch of us at Sauvie's Island, a big dyke picnic by the river. I'd been drinking beer, arguing with Brooke, singing off-key with whoever had brought a guitar. I stuck my head in the cool green river water every few minutes to douse the fire inside my skull.

It was my buddy Flanner who got my attention, because she usually drank as much as I did. Or so I'd thought. She looked at me and said, "You're fucked up Olivia." She didn't laugh. And the point came home to me when the picnic was all over and I unpacked the trunk and found a collapsing sixpack with three full warm brown bottles in it. I said, "What's this?

Flanner told me we were out of beer hours ago."

Brooke answered gently as if breaking bad news, "Flanner hid the last of the beer hours ago because she could see you had had too much."

Years later, there I was, walking up the last rise in the park, shaking my head and finally agreeing that I had had too much. I lined up Rachel with my other informants, remembered her at the Hungry Puffin, tapping my wineglass and asking me, "Are you in control or is this?"

Believe me, I didn't want to know all of this. But the indicators were all there. Kathleen had finally put it in so many dangerous words the night before.

Between the trees at the edge of the park I saw the great gray Pacific. I ran down the hill and under the highway to the beach. There was nowhere left to go. I didn't know what was beyond the edge of everywhere I'd been. I felt like I was going to have to jump off a cliff and learn to fly. The ocean kept pounding in. All of this was familiar in spite of its strangeness. Like running to meet a long lost twin. Like the way the ocean never missed a beat in my heart no matter how long I was away.

A few other Sunday stragglers wandered the beach, politely circumnavigating each other's sight lines. I sat on the soft sand. The waves sighed. I sighed. The breeze tousled my hair. I leaned on my elbows and tried to think things through, though it all kept going in circles.

I couldn't quit. I'd found that out. I couldn't cut down. I was out of control. So I had to quit. An absolute commitment. With all my strength. And help. Kathleen had told me it doesn't get better. It gets worse.

I knew that, too, because I remembered Malcolm and his kitchen floor full of bottles. I could hear him again saying, "Don't ask me that." I suddenly understood the smile he'd always faced his losses with, the odd satisfaction in it. Every loss left room for more booze. Until he couldn't quit because it was his whole life. His whole self. What would he be without it?

122

And me? I tried to imagine myself without alcohol. It made me shiver to be alone with the airless pit of fear that the noise of drinking covers. After all these years, I was afraid there would be nothing there when I got down to plain self. It would be just like starting over.

I pulled my head into my hands, my elbows into my belly. Drinking filled so many spaces in my day, my head, my heart. If I quit, I'd be left facing all those empty spaces without even the laughing anaesthetic to help.

It reminded me of something Judith's mother, Barbara, had said one spring day in Missoula after it was all over with Malcolm. Judith was in graduate school in the East, then. And Leo had been dead seven years, but still, somehow, was always with us. Barbara understood a lot of things I never knew how to explain. We drove out into the country, green wheatfields flying past the old Volvo windows. Her voice sad and knowing as the quarter hour chime, she said, "We always want to leave them better than we find them. But Malcolm will never be happy until he faces himself. You can't do that for him."

No, but I can do it for myself, I thought. That's enough to keep me busy.

The ocean shook its white locks at me and I laughed in the center of my pain. Absurd, but true, there was no choice. If I didn't quit, I'd have no choice. That only left one choice. Now Malcolm, I thought, there was a man who wouldn't give up drinking to save his life. That was the difference between us.

Not such a big difference up to this point. I'd been paying so little attention to what I needed to do, I could have destroyed myself, too. It's easier than you think.

I gave in to the obvious. It was exhausting to think of what I had to do. I didn't know what it was going to be like, except that it was going to be the hardest thing I'd ever do.

I lay down and rested while the breeze blew gritty sand over my eyelids. The roar of the ocean curled up beside me and I slept, unafraid, for a moment, of the changes. I woke up again who knows how much later. I remembered what I was going to do. I felt a little stronger to do it. With a little help from my friends.

I walked back into my apartment house just as the sun hit the treetops. I didn't want to let the day go. But I did.

I turned on the space heater and changed out of my damp clothes. As I was dripping a cup of coffee, I saw Rachel's face in the steam.

I called her and said, "I've decided to quit drinking."

I felt like I was announcing a birth. She matched my high spirits with her congratulations and chuckled as if she were bubbling over.

"When?"

"Next Saturday."

"Why Saturday?"

"I need a little time to say goodbye. Bad as it's been, I feel like I'm losing an old friend."

"That makes sense," she said, which surprised me because it sounded pretty crazy to me. Then she said, "But what made you decide now?"

"I have a friend who pointed a few things out. She quit. She can help."

"That's great. What about your lover?"

"We split up."

"I'm sorry."

I was surprised to find myself smiling. Maybe I couldn't have done this with Brooke. Maybe there was a lot of good to come out of all that pain of losing her. I said, "I honestly believe it's working out for the best."

"And the city?"

"I hate it." I was still grinning. "But I have a commitment to this job in the hospital, now. And anyway, it's important having Kathleen here. My friend. How about you? Are you still happy with the ocean and your music and your grandmother's house?"

"Very," she said. She sighed.

I said, "It would be nice to see you again."

"That's just what I was thinking. When you get tired of the city, remember, there's room for you here."

"I'm already tired of the city. But I have to stay a while. Do you want to come down?"

She laughed, "No. But I'll be here."

I was flying, but scared to trust that. I said, "I think you're a dream."

"I am that. But you'll see me on your phone bill."

"You don't know how true that is."

"I just have this feeling that, if you do your work and I do mine, we'll get a chance to finish our conversation."

"I hope so." I felt stupid to have left her there. But then I saw that I'd had to go through what I'd gone through before I could even think of going back. As usual, she'd already figured that out.

I said, "So, you're making some good music?"

She said, "I am. How about your stories?"

"They're talking to me, just a little."

"Great. I'm glad you're doing what you need to do. I'd be very happy to see you one of these days."

"Me too, Rachel." I was about to hang up when I remembered to say, "Hey, thanks for getting me started."

"You're welcome, Olivia. Good luck."

I waited until Friday to tell Kathleen because I didn't want her to think I was letting her tell me what to do. All week I felt like I was saving up a surprise for her. Not that I didn't know the gift was to myself. But sometimes I'd look at her and laugh for no good reason.

When I did tell her, she looked at me seriously, then hugged me and said, "Girl, you're a hero."

That's a big word, hero. That's what they call you when you've wrestled with death and come back alive. I saw how hard it had been for her. I felt a chill at how far I had to go. How powerful the opposition was. It made me really glad Kathleen was there. I hugged her again and said, "You are my hero, no fooling." Then we laughed.

Friday evening, April 1, 1981, I stopped at Maud's and drank my last Dos Equis with a lime. It was eight-thirty, bar time. The beer was already starting to taste not that good. In a lot of ways, I wasn't going to miss it. I toasted my own freedom ecstatically, crazily. To the bartender with the shortstop arms I said, "This is my last drink ever."

She said, "That's great," in the same tone she always said, "Another?"

I could tell she didn't believe me. How many times had she heard that one before? How many times had I, myself, said it?

But the brew knew. It wept on the bar and kissed me wetly goodbye.

CHAPTER SEVEN

Saturday morning the pipes clanged in my apartment and the sun shone on my sea green walls. I woke with a pleasant prickling under my skin. I pulled my sheets into my duffel bag thinking, this is the laundry of my first sober day. And I wondered that the man who tended the machines in the bustling neighborhood laundromat looked at me as if I were the same person I'd been the week before. I smoothed out the old blue comforter thinking, I am making the bed of my first sober day.

I walked through the eucalyptus trees on the Panhandle. Every step felt new. I made up a list of things I would do with the time and energy freed from this long entanglement: poetry, politics, walks by the water, long talks with friends, play with children.

I met Kathleen at the Pork Store for the first breakfast of my sober life. We toasted each other with black coffee in a ceremony as exciting as any with champagne. She said, "Here's to Olivia, who loves fresh starts and can't turn down a dare. May your stubbornness serve you well."

I had the strange sensation that the next step higher was one that started on solid ground. Kathleen grinned and gave me this eyebrows raised look that I knew meant, "Are we in this together or what?" I nodded and she grinned again. I saw that she was going to be there when I needed her and I could hardly bear how happy that made me. She patted my hand and looked like she was going to dance because she knew we could do it.

The grits, which Kathleen had taught me to eat, were warm and buttery. The coffee sparkled in heavy white mugs. A change was already started in my gut like high tide turning to the long roll out to sea.

After breakfast, I hugged her, almost wanting to shade my heart from the brightness of going that much further into everything. Then I walked toward home with the sunshine warming my arms. I wondered how completely the change in chemistry would change me.

I stopped at the corner grocery to buy an orange. I sat on the fender of a Volkswagen and put my thumb under the peel. There was the gift, the same old world with one less layer of numbness around it. The fruit was sweet.

The acacia tree in the next block had sprung a million yellow flowers even though it was hemmed in by concrete. My bag lady came up the sidewalk with her jacket tied around her waist, humming to herself in the sunshine. We had all come back from the dead. She didn't look at me or ask for anything. But I folded a five into her hand for good luck and walked on, jumping up to tap the sign hanging over the drugstore with great satisfaction.

Monday afternoon, the call button for Room 808 buzzed and lit up at my desk. I answered and heard the Go-Go's rocking softly in the background as Marna Thatcher asked for a fresh blanket. The nurses were busy, so I slipped into the kitchen and pulled a paper wrapped blanket out of the warmer. I put on a mask and went into 808.

Marna was a twenty-year-old, chemotherapy bald woman. She smiled shyly as I came in. I unfolded the blanket and asked, "How are you doing today?"

"Not so bad," she said. "I vomited all night, but this morning I slept."

"That's better then."

"I think I dreamed about dying."

"Oh?"

"I was swimming deeper and deeper in the ocean. It was dark green, and it was sort of wonderful. Not having to come back to the surface. I wasn't afraid."

She patted a square of sunlight on the bed. "I'm glad I'm still alive, though."

I said, "I'm glad, too."

Scott and Cindy Wells poked their heads around the door. Cindy, the seven-year-old, had received a marrow transplant two weeks before from her slightly older brother, Scott. Both wore masks to protect her from infection.

Cindy giggled, "Look what we've got."

Scott wheeled in a wheel chair with Cindy's big stuffed bunny sitting in it. They had taped an old I-V line and a hickman catheter to the bunny's chest, just like the one Cindy wore. And on his lap they had placed a smaller teddy bear.

"How is the patient doing?" I asked.

Scott pointed to a bandaid covering a betadine stain on the bunny's seat. "We had to do a bone marrow on him today."

"But he's feeling better," Cindy added. "And his labs are good."

I patted the bunny's furry face. "I'm glad to hear it. And he's in such good hands. I guess I'd better get back to the desk."

I looked at Marna and saw tears in her eyes even as she laughed at the kids and said, "You two are such a pair of goofballs."

That night I dreamed of the burnt-out corpse of the woman in the emerald evening gown. Nicotine colored skin hung from her arms. She carried a bouquet spilling gardenias. She wouldn't look at me.

I said, "Come to work with me tomorrow. I want you to meet the people there and see how much they want to live even if they go through incredible pain to do it."

Her voice was like a scratched old victrola record being cranked slowly. She said, "Pain. Pah! Everyone has pain. But can you handle pleasure?"

I woke up laughing a little. But I thought of this dream one evening at the Women's Building about a month later. I was looking at a bulletin board and a conference brochure caught my eye, a slick, folded, black and white piece of paper lingering in one corner overdressed and out of place among the felt-penned notices of potlucks and support groups. I crouched close enough to read that the National Caucus of Feminist Historians was meeting at the Sheraton the first week of June.

I untacked the announcement and stood with the image of Alice Benedict, the lean, sharp-faced classicist from Portland State, spinning across my nerves. The last time I'd seen her was at a sorrowful defiant party at the end of a season's gay rights lobbying. She'd stood in a corner in white flannel pants and a navy blazer holding forth after three martinis.

I read the brochure in my hand. Between the lines of predictable plenary sessions and specialized groups, I could see Alice Benedict treading silently across the plush hotel lobby with a paper to present in a manila envelope under her arm and the arguments in its defense lining up like a drill team on the exercise field of her mind.

I folded onto a sagging sofa and urged my imagination to behave. I focused on the dry description of the conference until I reached the final event, a women's dance in the hotel ballroom with a Latina band from Oakland.

I could drop around, I thought. It should be good music. I might run into Alice, each of us crossing the floor with some other purpose. We might both be alone and restless. Certainly I would be. Alice would be surprised to see me. We'd recount our lives since we've last seen each other in cascades of words that never catch up with the years. We wouldn't dance — Alice doesn't. But Alice might very well say, "Why don't you and I get a bottle of gin and go somewhere."

Yes, I thought. That, if anything, is what Alice would say, in a voice that sounds as if she is proposing a practically patriotic manuever, but also with a conspiratorial fastening of the eyes. And wasn't that the only place Alice and I ever really met — the bee-line for the bar? Weren't we the two who agreed that a good meeting should always have plenty of beer? Didn't we share the same territory, never too far from the punch?

If I could say yes, we might even touch as we never had, Alice being away from home, me being on my own, the whole thing being less complicated than ever before. But I did not think Alice would be pleased if I said then, as I would have to, "Well, the fact is, I've given up drinking."

Alice would bluster, as if it were a joke. "Give up drinking? Heavens no, my dear. Give up righteousness. Give up your best friend's secrets. But don't give up drinking."

What connection would be left? I did not think Alice Benedict would go off with me to share a bottle of Calistoga. And I couldn't imagine myself saying, "Let's skip the gin and just go somewhere."

I was all too familiar with the approach of suggesting a drink when what you really want is contact. It's a way of denying that sex or friendship or any touch that allays loneliness is the point. Drinking is the point. The rest comes along sideways, staggering, unintended. When I was drunk, I didn't have to put myself on the line. I could say, the gin made me do it. I could say, I didn't mean to want anything.

I remembered how I used to bring a bottle of wine to a woman as a way of saying I wanted to make love with her. And if she brought a bottle of wine, too, that would be a very good sign. And by the time we'd finished both bottles of wine, we might as well have hit each other over the head with them. There was no place to go but bed. We couldn't walk enough to go anywhere else if we wanted to. We had no choice but to cling to one another. Wine was such a strong-arm tactic.

I had never made love sober before. I was amazed at how shy I had become. I was going to have to learn the whole thing all over again and I could see it was going to be a very self-conscious project. What, I wondered, had been the point of doing it with a load of anaesthetic anyway? Easier to take risks, for sure. But can you feel it?

I punched the thumbtack into the conference schedule again. I was lonely. I did want to make contact. But I was taking it easy, too. I could almost hear Diana Ross reminding me, you can't hurry love.

I didn't think much that first spring about the implications of what I was doing. I didn't consider myself an alcoholic. I just wanted to quit drinking quietly and get Kathleen off my back. I didn't want to admit how hard it was. Though my pride in the accomplishment should have given me away. I'm not sure how much of the lingering fog that year was in the air and how much inside my head. I meditated a lot. Took a lot of hot baths. Kathleen tells me I cried a lot.

One morning I dreamed I was in the courtyard at Maud's and the strawberry blonde bartender had brought me a shot of Wild Turkey. I swallowed it and the lining of my nose screamed. I could taste it. And I remembered what a mistake it was. How hard I'd worked on those months of sobriety. How I was back at square one. It was mournful, like losing someone I loved.

When I told Kathleen, she rubbed my neck and said, "Yeah. That's a bad dream. It happens. That's part of it."

I said, "You don't know how grateful I was to wake up and realize it was only a dream."

She smiled a little sadly and said, "Don't I?"

I shook my head and shrugged and said, "Maybe you do."

The next day, at work, we sent Marna Thatcher home. I've never seen anyone more ecstatic to be wearing street clothes and walking away from that hospital bed. She hugged me and said she'd visit when she came back for her annual check-up. She put her walkman headset on her ears and snapped her fingers and rocked away down the hall.

As I was taking Marna's chart apart, a delivery woman brought an arrangement of pink roses and baby's breath for Cindy Wells' parents. I said, "Oh, Okay," and signed for them. Then I called Intensive Care, because we'd transferred Cindy down there with pneumonia and cardiac complications which put her on a respirator and a heart monitor.

A few minutes later, the ICU ward clerk called me back. "The Wells' can't handle the roses, Olivia. They're staying here day and night now, and we don't allow flowers on the floor. Mrs. Wells said to tell you to keep them."

I sighed. It was a hard way to get roses. They weren't really allowed on 8W, either. But I said, "Okay. Tell them thanks. And I hope things get better."

I stored the roses in the locker room for the rest of my shift and then carried them home where they looked kind of funny in my pleasantly bare apartment.

One weekend, my old buddy Flanner came down from Portland with this other friend of ours, Lisa. After we found room to hang coats, stash suitcases and roll out sleeping bags, we christened my apartment the world's tiniest lesbian hostel. I opened a bottle of sparkling cider without feeling the least bit satirical. They changed into their out-of-towners out on the town clothes, and we walked arm in arm through the fog to a bar on Fillmore where I'd heard this woman Rosalie was singing wonderful scat.

We watched Rosalie testing microphones in Salvation Army lace-up little old lady shoes and an Egyptian crown of frizzed out red hair. We checked out the dykely certainty in the turn of her hips and the way she carried on with groups of women clustered at tables around the room. It was basically a straight place and the people who ran it liked the intense intricate rhythms Rosalie sang. No one could tell what she was actually saying because it was all be-boppa-boosh-do-wah. But we had our own interpretation.

Flanner was ordering vodka Collinses, Lisa had white wine, and I had bottled water. We all wrapped nervous smiles around our glasses. It had taken me a while to learn it was okay to sit in a bar without a beer in my hand. The part of me that had always been a regular was dying away, the part of me that had bought drink after drink to pay dues to the club as if the bar was the source of all my music and laughter and I owed it everything I had. Still, I could see the classic barstool dyke with a shot glass always in front of her, representing her inalienable right to the space she occupied. How she would turn and look at you as if to say, did you come here to drink, or what?

But what was really in front of me was a gray haired frayed overcoat man with a whiskey between his thumb and forefinger, standing next to the bandstand singing raw ragged nonsense against Rosalie's high-pitched slides. I was embarrassed for him and myself, because I'd done that before, not understanding that what I had inside my head was not what came out of my mouth. Not seeing that I was in the way of the show everyone came to see.

Rosalie turned and bent down close to him and sang right between his eyes, "If you don't sit down quiet, man, I can't get on with my song."

His bleary eyes took her for someone else and his grizzly bear shoulders shrugged. He sat down. I was relieved. I ordered another Calistoga. Rosalie wound up her first set with "Wild Women Don't Get the Blues."

Lisa meandered to the bathroom wide-eyed over all the tables of women on her way. Flanner leaned on one elbow with her eyes red and warm on me. She said, "It's great about you quitting. I don't see why we can't enjoy going out like this. As long as you don't think we're awful now."

I shook my head.

Flanner stared at her fingers as if they were going to dissolve into the glass she was holding. She said, "To tell you the truth, I'm worried about Lisa. You can hear that cough. So much smoking and drinking and not sleeping or eating right. Almost like someone who wants to hurt herself. Maybe it would help if you talked to her."

"Maybe it would." I rolled a piece of lime along my teeth.

When Lisa came back, Flanner went to the bathroom. Lisa turned my glass of water all the way around and said, "You're amazing."

I shrugged and ducked my head.

Lisa pulled a curl out of her new harpo perm and leaned close to say, "I wish you would say something to Flanner, though, while we're here. She's been drinking a whole lot more than she used to. And she's depressed. Broke down crying in Chinatown today for no reason."

I shook my head wondering if I was hearing this all right.

Lisa put two fingers on my wrist pulse and whispered, "Don't tell her I said anything. She thinks I'm putting her down if I try to talk about it."

I said okay as Flanner rejoined us and the piano rattled and Rosalie turned up in the red spotlight singing "Ball and Chain."

Kathleen edited my writing, a lot like Judith had done when we were kids. She saw my attempts at poetry, a couple of reviews and several drafts of my first short story. When I thought I had finally finished that story, I handed it to her nervously at lunch. That evening I took the elevator up to the half-lab half-office on the twelfth floor where she worked. I paced around and looked out the window at the ocean and the pastel colored houses while Kathleen typed the last footnotes on her professor's latest article.

The clatter stopped and I said, "Well?"

I have no patience with anything but the matter at hand at a time like that.

Kathleen looked up for a few seconds knowing it was too important and vulnerable a moment to tease. Then she started grinning proudly at me and said, "Well, it's great, that's what."

She would always say something like that, but still it relieved me to hear it. Kathleen packed things from her desk into her canvas briefcase, slightly used manila envelopes, an empty yoghurt cup. She handed me my story. Across the top she'd written, "It's a dance!"

I put my arm around her shoulder as we walked to the elevator and said, "God, I'm glad you like it."

She said, "You worked hard on this. You did what you needed to do. It should be good."

As we walked down the hill toward home, I watched the Cole Valley women in the hardware store, the laundromat, the doorway of the bar. Once or twice Kathleen got stopped by a poster or notice tacked up along the way. There are life stories posted on the telephone poles of Haight-Ashbury, and Kathleen would get caught in print as surely as if it were a butterfly net.

At the Chatanooga Cafe, she ordered a chocolate ice cream cone and I ordered raspberry. She asked, "How can you eat that berry stuff? Don't the seeds get caught in your teeth?"

I shrugged and laughed and said, "No."

She said, "How come?"

I said, "It's one of life's mysteries," and we walked on. After her cone was gone, Kathleen started studying the sidewalk and I started wondering what she was working up to. She said, "There's just one thing that bothers me at the end of your story."

"What's that?"

"The wine."

The air around me thinned as I thought about the three glasses of wine at the end of my story. I said, "That's the way it was."

I was happier than ever about having quit drinking. But I wasn't sure how to handle my past self, the life this story came out of. I didn't want to censor it to fit some kind of sober party line. And it was the only kind of life I knew much about so far. I said, "That's what this character would do — at that time."

"Does she have to?"

"Yeah she does. Those glasses of wine mark a progression toward the insight the whole thing ends up on. It's *in vino veritas*, the truth in the wine."

"Don't you think that's romanticizing drinking?"

137

"Don't you think there's some truth to it? Aren't there some things that come clearer when you're a little ways out there after a few glasses of wine?"

"I think it seems that way when you're drinking. But have you ever listened sober to what those insights come down to?"

We stopped at the corner where my way continued down Cole and Kathleen's turned up Haight. Kathleen shifted her briefcase under her arm and looked steadily up at me. She said, "Think about it, Olivia. What really happened to that character that night?"

I frowned at the corner of the brick wall. "She went out to a bar and got drunk and went home."

"And what did she think?"

"She didn't think anything. She felt sorry for herself. She didn't want to think. Well, shit. Maybe there is something dishonest about putting a sober insight into a drunk's mouth."

I rubbed my head and pulled at the hair at the back of my neck. "If I have to cut out either the wine or the insight, the wine will have to go."

"Of course." Kathleen waited like she had nothing better to do in the whole world than to stand on that street corner and find out what I thought.

I sighed. "I don't know, Kathleen. I just don't know if I can get the feeling I want without those glasses of wine."

Kathleen hugged me and said, "That's the question isn't it?"

The next week we readmitted Marna Thatcher to 8W. She had CMV in her central nervous sytem. Her hair had grown back like a plush movie theater seat. She still had her verve, but it was slowed by the methadone cocktails, and sometimes she talked to people who weren't there. I was not happy to see her.

I dreamed of my nightmare woman in her green dress again. Short blue blonde hair greasily combed into spitcurls.

138

She still wouldn't look at me. But I smelled something like blown-off day-after whiskey breath, or formaldehyde. She said to me, "What have you got there, you fool? Don't you know nothing lasts? You might as well throw it in the flames now and watch it flash."

She embraced me like smoke, her arms sagged around my neck and her head rested on my shoulder. She whispered, "You know what we know. You can always come back."

I woke up terrified. I called Kathleen and she met me for coffee. She said, "You're doing great, Liv. You've got an addiction and it doesn't want to let you go. But it wouldn't fight so hard if it wasn't losing ground. It will get better. Can you hold on?"

She looked out from under her bangs at me. I nodded. She said, "You tell me if it gets to be too hard."

The last Sunday in June I wandered down to the Gay Pride March where half a million people were parading along Market Street in the sunshine. I loved the Dykes on Bikes roaring by, and the Parents of Gays sending that ripple of sentimentality through the crowd wherever they passed. My favorite character was the bearded fellow in the Glinda-the-good-witch getup: crinoline skirts, glittering crown and wand, and a sign around his neck that said, "It takes balls to be a fairy."

I stood on the sidewalk appreciating the constant movement of people in and out of the surging dragon. Then I saw the group of gay men and lesbians behind the "Clean and Sober" banner. We all shouted and I shivered at how much had changed for me. The year before, in Portland, I had applauded when the Clean and Sober contingent passed by. I'd thought how courageous their statement was in a community that values booze so highly as an instrument of seduction and communion. But I'd felt hypocritical cheering that year, because the possibility of being sober and proud had seemed as remote as the possibility of

139

visiting another planet. The year before, the fear of alienating my drinking sisters, missing the party in some basic way, had kept me from even contemplating that incredible reach. But there I was a year later. I had landed on the far planet. And seeing that banner made it feel a lot more like home.

A wave of excitement came down the street with the women's percussion band, sixty women dressed in white and playing drums and tambourines, a salsa march. I fell in ahead of the band and behind the Women's Health Care Collective who wore red T-shirts and held up plastic speculums. There were other women with familiar faces dancing there. One carried a small child. The rhythm pulsed through us in a heartbeat and hip beat and backbone unrolling, music breathing passage of a small dyke nation down the main drag. As my feet pounded, anger and fear and despair drained, and fire flowed up out of the trembling earth. I found myself grinning and thinking, I used to drink to dance. And now I dance to heal. I thought, if I believed in the goddess, I'd thank her for the dance, and the motion that feels so good even in the middle of the street while the asphalt heats up and the towers tower. Salt sweat ran down my face and I thanked her anyway, because it made so much sense to have someone to thank.

I was very high and very dry when I turned in to the Civic Center Square thirty blocks later. I would have pawned my shoes for a drink. Large placards on the nearest wall proclaimed, "Cold Beer." And I felt like I would cry if there wasn't anything better than that at the end of the long march for freedom and pride.

I started to look for Kathleen, who was minding an anti-nuke booth with her lover, Joan. I was working up to a scream if I didn't find a glass of water soon.

All of this reminded me of a conversation Kathleen and I had the week before, when I was feeling edgy about going to a party. I'd said, "These are the times I used to drink: when I was bored, when I was nervous, when I was meeting new people.

Now if I'm nervous, especially about being tempted to drink, I dance. So, my terrible fantasy is that I dance half the night and then I'm dying of thirst and there's nothing in the house but cold beer and chilled wine. What circle of hell is that?"

Kathleen laughed at me and said, "This house — does it have running water?"

When I finally found Kathleen, she rescued me knowingly with a jug of cold juice. I leaned on her and watched the rest of the great gay parade coming in. I said, "You know, when I used to drink, I was always thirsty."

"I know," she said, "It dehydrates you."

"Malcolm used to make fun of me when I'd wake up with my tongue curling. He'd say, 'Why are you thirsty? You were drinking all night.' It's a mean joke isn't it, once you finally get it?"

Kathleen nodded. I said, "Half the reason I drank all those years was because I was so thirsty."

I mostly stayed away from bars, at first, because it didn't feel safe. Thank god San Francisco is a great city of cafes. But one August evening after sunning in Dolores Park all day, I dropped into Scott's Pit. The smell of beer-soaked carpet and hot popcorn oil took me back unpleasantly.

I sat in a booth with some people I knew a little. They got up to play pool and I found myself looking at a pale green bottle of champagne left smoking on the table. I turned it around to read the label. Ugh. Stuff I would have avoided even if I were still drinking.

A large woman in a black leather jacket, black curls, cartoon T-shirt, jeans and boots, grabbed the bottle by the neck, turned up her head and chugged it. I wanted to defend myself and say, "I wasn't about to drink it."

But that was beside the point. I looked up at her throat and intestines glugging the champagne like the dream boa snake that

141

can swallow anything and rest until it digests. Somehow I had thought our enormous appetites would have saved us. Our ability to swallow so much.

I thought of the things that had helped me get sober, stubbornness, aikido, meditation, massage, seeing what would happen if I didn't, getting at it while I still could. Most of all, having friends who liked me sober.

All of that seemed like nothing against the pain of a fifth of booze, even champagne, going into a woman's gut. The way drinking is like dying, tearing the picture away until you pass out and wake up somewhere else feeling lucky to have survived the night. Or maybe in a sweat because nothing has changed, your bills are still due, you don't like yourself any better, you've run your friends off, your head aches, and even booze disappoints you.

I remembered all of this. And I walked out of Scott's feeling lucky, and thinking, sometimes you just have to pick your pain.

All that was left of my nightmare by then was a voice the next morning. "None of us would really change what we've done," she whispered in my ear.

I put my hands behind my head and stared up at the ceiling. For the first time in a long time, I thought of Judith's father, Leo. I thought, he, for example, didn't really prefer to shoot himself. He would have lived if he could have. It suddenly struck me kind of funny how Malcolm had sat on the floor the day of Leo's memorial, drinking whiskey for a man who would have still been alive if he could have quit drinking whiskey. That had been the same day I'd first understood that life is a choice. Now here I was making that choice every day.

For a moment, as I started breakfast, I felt haunted in a very different way. It was almost as if Leo were behind me, nodding, saying, "Good. You're doing good. I'm proud of you."

142

Of course he wasn't really there. It was just a thought, but it helped me remember why I was doing what I was doing, and I was grateful for that. I watched my knife buttering the toast and realized that I was growing into my own blue-veined hands.

One cold blue October morning, I walked out of the locker room at work wearing a fresh set of scrubs. A Duke Ellington tune bounced around in my head. I'd had a day off and I was disoriented when I looked at the assignment board. There were suddenly too many empty rooms. One of the night nurses sat at a desk doing her charts. I asked, "What happened?"

She looked up. "Marna Thatcher expired at 5:30 this morning." I heard the quiet on the ward and I could hardly believe I had practically been whistling a moment before.

She went on to explain the other discharges and transfers, but my attention had fixed on how sharp the orange leaves outside become when the girl down the hall can't see them anymore.

The routine of death was fairly simple. I organized Marna's chart to go to Medical Records one last time. There was a problem about the autopsy and a mortician to entertain. As I typed Marna's address on the Death Certificate, I wondered in what sense it could still be called her address.

I had to track down Dr. Deems, who was on call, but had not been present at Marna's death. I found her busy with another patient on another floor. She resented having to sign the Death Certificate for another doctor's patient, and I had to explain that she was the only one available. She took it and sat down at the desk while I waited.

She asked, "Was there an autopsy?"

I said, "No."

She filled in a few words and then stopped, tapping her pen on the blotter. "Immediate cause of death?"

143

"I don't know." I was struck with how little I understood of the causes of death and the causes of life.

"Did she stop breathing?" Deems asked.

"I don't know. I wasn't there." This seemed an absurd question. Of course she stopped breathing. We wouldn't be writing a Death Certificate if she were still breathing.

Deems wrote "respiratory arrest" in a tiny precise hand in the immediate cause of death rectangle.

I walked back to my own floor feeling silly over how the whole hospital was unequal to the most basic questions. So much technology, research, care; and in the end, people die because they stop breathing.

Marna's primary nurse sat at the front desk, contemplative, angry. "I'm trying to understand why this one got to me. I've lost patients before."

I shrugged sympathetically. Marna's death was certainly getting to me.

Other patients and their families sat quietly, picking at their lunches, looking out their windows at the white noon light.

The pharmacist listened to a football game. When it was over, he let me set the radio on my desk. I couldn't get a classical station, but found some jazz to listen to while I worked on lab requests and reports. One patient's wife walked by and said, "That's pretty upbeat." I wasn't sure whether she meant the music was inappropriate on the day of Marna's death. I compromised and turned it down low, thinking life was too short to do without a little piano, a little saxophone.

When Kathleen showed up to walk me home, I told her all about it. I said, "When I was drinking, it never seemed like time or death could touch me. You know, you're even astounded to look up and see that it's closing time. Lately I feel like a bundle of sticks and tubes that can't last long."

Kathleen slipped her hand around my arm and didn't say anything.

I said, "I'm not sure I wanted to know this."

She nodded. Then she bent down and picked up a green marble from the sidewalk. Cat's eye, I thought, as she handed me the scratched globe that had somehow lost its child. I slipped it in my pocket and my heart felt warm.

I said, "It all comes together, doesn't it? Love and death and beauty and time and change."

She rubbed my back.

I took a deep painful breath of the cooling evening and said, "I guess this is the year we decided it was better to feel the hurt than not to feel at all."

She said, "Yeah. It was too creepy the other way."

When I got home, I reached into the back of my closet and found the canvas covered case there by touch. I had a sad laugh remembering how my mother used to sing off-key lullabies to me. How I can't sing either. But she did give me a flute with a beautiful voice. I remembered one time even perfect pitch Judith had the patience to play a duet with me. I softly clacked the silver keys, familiar, in the end, as my own bones. I thought, as I often had before, what a long sight better instrument it was than I would ever be musician.

I remembered a piece of Rachel's song, then a ballad that reminded me of Judith, then a phrase that was just a piece of music. It was only warm air and silver after all. But that night it seemed to me that life was nothing more than a stream of breath and whatever you can make of that.

ABOUT THE AUTHOR

Marian Michener was born in Boston in 1952. She received an MA in English/Creative Writing from San Francisco State University in 1984. She presently lives in Seattle and works for the AIDS Training Project of the University of Washington. Her short stories have appeared in *Common Lives/Lesbian Lives, Rag Times, Out and About, Crossing the Mainstream,* and *The Guide.* This is her first novel. She has been clean and sober since 1981.